A River of Seasons
By: Ron Shepherd

Global Video Marketing
& Graphic Design
Publishing Division

Second printing
Email: peaceriverbooks@ronshepherd.com
Website: www.ronshepherd.com


ISBN: 0-9769455-4-1
PUBLISHED BY GLOBAL VIDEO MARKETING
PUBLISHING DIVISION
www.globalvideomarketing.com
Minnesota


Printed in the United States of America

*To my wife Janie*
*with love*

# TABLE OF CONTENTS

CHAPTER 1    THE FIRE

CHAPTER 2    THE TRIP HOME

CHAPTER 3    CHRISTMAS ON THE RIVER

CHAPTER 4    THE LOGGING CAMPS

CHAPTER 5    FIRST ADVENTURE

CHAPTER 6    LIFE ON THE RIVER

CHAPTER 7    SAM'S CAMP

CHAPTER 8    MOUNTAIN LOGGING

CHAPTER 9    FALL ON THE BIGFORK

CHAPTER 10   SCOOTER

CHAPTER 11   THE HUNT

# CHAPTER 1
## THE FIRE

The weathered looking man dipped his canoe paddle quietly into the dark water of the Bigfork River and pulled. As he lifted it to repeat the motion, water fell from the paddle into the river making a soft tinkling sound. Wil Morgan wore a wide-brimmed hat and had a neatly trimmed beard that was a broad mixture of salt and pepper. His red and black plaid shirt gave him the look of a lumberjack which he indeed was.

He looked ahead down river and saw the first rays of sunshine peek from behind the cattails. It was an unusually warm morning and the colors of fall lit his world up brightly as the sun rose higher in the sky. The yellows of the birch trees and the reds of the sugar maples made the trip down river to the General Store one that he always enjoyed. Such simple pleasures were to his liking at this age, nothing to get his heart racing. He liked the little things like the smell of morning coffee over a campfire or the sound of a loon's lonesome call on a moonlit night. He had spent his life on this river and knew each bend and beaver lodge for many miles. The vast expanse of the Bigfork River Valley was his back yard, the place he called home.

He was paddling close to the river bank and saw a large clump of ripe raspberries hanging close to the water. He paddled closer to get at his breakfast. He stayed there for a while just enjoying the taste of nature's finest berries.

He heard a soft "woof" from not too far away and knew that a bear was near by, also eating her breakfast. Then he thought of the possibility that she may have cubs so decided that he had eaten enough breakfast for now. A canoe filled with an ill tempered sow didn't appeal to him. He pushed off and resumed his course.

As he continued down stream, he saw a wisp of black smoke rising off to the east. He watched carefully as he paddled, and as he got closer his pace quickened some. The only people that lived in that area were the Anderson's and they wouldn't have a fire this early in the morning. Soon he was able to smell the smoke and knew immediately that it was a house fire.      The canoe hit the river bank near the house and Wil ran up the hill toward the smoke. What he saw was a smoldering pile of debris that no longer resembled a home that held a family of five good people. The grass had burned for several yards around the pile of ashes indicating an extremely hot fire.

He looked around the yard for any clue that the family had escaped and he found nothing. Then from the edge of the woods near a shed, he heard someone speak his name. It was a soft sound like that of a child. He hurried toward the voice and within very few steps saw the forms of two young children huddled together, shaking from cold and fear. Young Sam and his sister Missy had survived the fire.They ran to Wil and held onto him, not saying anything. Wil was a friend to the whole family and he knew the children well from the day of their birth.

After a time of hard sobbing and tears, young Sam related to Wil what had happened. It seems that during the night, someone threw something on fire through the window and the whole place burned very quickly. His Ma and Pa had gotten the older two children out, but went back in to get the baby and didn't come out again. He had heard his Mother scream and then the whole house went up in flames.

Wil looked down at Missy and asked her if she was alright. She looked up at Wil and didn't say anything. Her eyes looked like the fire of life itself had gone out. He spoke to her again and she stared at Wil with no expression and no words. He figured that she had seen too much on this dreadful day. Who could have done such a thing to a good, hard working family!

There were some burns on Sam's hands and Wil wrapped them with strips of cloth from the clothes line. The two children were still shaking after an hour and Wil thought he better get them to the General Store where someone could care for them.

He walked over to the barn and turned out the livestock. There were two milk cows and a pair of draft horses. They could fare well for themselves until someone could come for them. Wil got the children into the canoe and started off down river toward the small town, with little Missy sitting on the bottom of the canoe between Wil's legs. She had a firm grip on Wil and wouldn't let go of him. She still made no sound. Sam was a big kid and he knew well how to paddle a canoe. He sat up front and matched strokes with Wil, paddling strongly. He had been a good helper to his father and mother and at times his parents would leave for days with him in charge, taking good care of his sister. He was growing up hard and lean, the way you had to if you would survive Northern Minnesota. It was a tough land and if you couldn't handle it, you went back to the ground early.

Wil had lived many years on the river and prospered from his hard work. He either worked the logging camps or farmed. In the winter he trapped in his spare time or fished. When times were tough, he went back to the logging camps. He tried to stay away from them if he could, since it meant that his wife was left alone all winter. He loved her far too much for that.

This was his home, all of it, the river, the bogs, the lakes, the big pines and the swamps. He knew it all and used it to suit himself. The animals were his as well. He trapped otter, beaver and muskrats. He hunted the caribou, the moose and deer. He fought with the roving packs of wolves that tried to take his livestock or his life. He would trap them or kill them outright if the opportunity presented itself. It was a tough land and to get to his age, he had to be a hard man.

The canoe glided along quietly but the colors of the leaves and the enjoyment he had felt earlier had dimmed. Now his mind raced with thoughts of the children and what they would do. He thought of what kind of a man would burn out a family in the middle of the night. This would have to be reported to the authorities. Sometimes a young buck from up near Redby would cause some trouble, but murder was out of the question. It was more likely a white man from one of the camps. These were hard times and men came from far and wide to earn cash money. Robbery wasn't the reason either, because young Sam would have seen something. This was a puzzle to Wil and the authorities would probably never figure it out.

The canoe rounded the last curve before the falls and Wil saw the town in the distance. He pulled the canoe in by the bank near the General Store and got out holding young Missy closely. They walked up the hill and into the store.

"Well, what do you have here Wil?" asked Milo the storekeeper.

"It's bad news we got today Milo. The Andersons got burned out and these two kids are all that's left of the family."

"Ann! Come quick," yelled Milo.

In just a moment, Milo's wife Ann came into the store and saw the two kids, wretched looking and eyes full of fear. It looked like they wanted to run but didn't know which way to go. Ann gathered them up and took them to the house for cleaning and bandaging as needed. She washed them thoroughly and got new clothes from the store. In short order, they were resting with full bellies, trying to assess their situation. Young Sam said that he would take Missy and go back to their place to build a new house, but he was too young for such a thing. He had the will, but not the strength. There would have to be other arrangements made.

Later in the day, Milo, Ann and Wil sat outside on the porch of the house, trying to decide what to do with the new orphans. The children had said that there were no other relatives, so they were indeed orphans. Wil felt that it would be more than his wife could handle, even if they were the best kids in the world. Milo and Ann weren't all that old, but they didn't want to start all over, raising kids. They sat there in the fall sunshine trying to decide the fate of a pair of nice kids that didn't deserve to be made orphans, especially at such a young age. Ann figured that they could stay with them for a couple weeks until they found a family that would take them in. Wil agreed and the meeting broke up. The kids didn't have much to say when they were told, but young Sam wanted to go home. He had plans to build the home again but his age was against him.

Wil got the supplies he came for and walked back down the hill to his canoe. As he pushed off from the bank, he saw little Missy standing in front of the General Store looking like she had lost her only friend. He waved to her, but there wasn't even any sign that she recognized him. He felt deep sorrow for the young girl. She went to sleep last night safe and secure with her ma and pa watching over her. Tonight she would be alone and her world would take a whole new course. He took a deep breath and started the trip back up river to his home. He pulled strongly on the paddle and the canoe responded slowly in the current.

# Chapter 2
## The Trip Home

After an hour's hard paddling, Wil was coming near to the Anderson's place, or at least what was left of it. He pulled in close to the bank and grabbed a handful of reeds to steady himself while he got out. Wil tied the canoe to a small tree and walked up the bank to where the house had been. He looked about and found nothing of interest – not even the bodies. The high temperatures had consumed them completely. The ashes were still too hot to dig into, but just the same, he looked for something, anything that he would be able to give to the kids as a remembrance. As he approached where the front door would have been, he noticed a large track in the ashes. It was from a hobnail boot, the kind that the loggers wear. His blood chilled at the thought that the murderer was still in the area. Had he come back to see that the job was done completely or had he come to search through the ruins for something of value? His tracks went through the cooler parts of the house and then went toward the woods.

Wil Morgan always carried a sidearm and today he was especially glad to have it. It was a Colt .45 and would do terrible damage if it had to. He followed the tracks into the woods. They seemed to be made by someone who didn't give a hoot if he was followed or not.

The tracks led around the edge of a swamp and back up into the big pines. The tracking was getting a bit more difficult as he went, but for the old woodsman, it was no trouble at all. He stopped for a breather and sat on a stump for a while. He took off his hat to wipe the sweat from his forehead. For a second he thought he heard something, and then the whole world went dark.

A large man with long black hair stood over Wil, ready to hit him again if he moved. He held a short chunk of pine with both hands, ready to strike a killing blow if he needed to. He rolled Wil over on his side and immediately recognized him from town. They had worked together in some of the lumber camps too. The man had been run off many times for stealing, and each time would find work at another of the many camps. The word was starting to get around though, and he was finding it harder all the time to get work and a meal.

He reached inside Wil's pocket and helped himself to the small roll of bills. All together, including his change, he had nearly $11.00, a great sum of money for the times. Then he unbuckled Wil's belt and took the Colt sidearm. He stared at Wil for a time, trying to decide if there was anything else of value he might steal. Wil was bleeding pretty bad from the back of his head and the murderer figured that he would never live anyway. He walked off like nothing had happened, leaving a clear trail if anyone had wanted to go after him.

After an hour or so, Wil awoke and felt a large lump on his head where the man had hit him. He staggered to his feet and his pants fell from him with no belt to hold them up. Over a couple feet to his left, he saw his belt, but the Colt was gone. He bent to pick it up and nearly passed out again. He sat on the ground trying to get his bearings. In a few minutes he was able to stand. He thought to go after the man, but now that he had lost his pistol, he would be at risk of losing his life too. A man that would try to kill a whole family wouldn't hesitate to kill a lone man. He thought for a while which direction he should go and decided to head back to the cabin, or at least what was left of it. When he got to the river bank, he washed his head wound and wrapped a bandage on the cut.

Then it was back to the pile of ashes. He looked hard for anything that might give a hint of who had done it. Then he saw it, a knife shining in the sun lying near the steps. He bent to pick it up and the first thing he noticed was that there were no burn marks on it. Then he noticed the initials BS on the handle. It was a small knife and extremely sharp. The unusual part was that it was sharp on both sides of the blade, the kind of knife a man like that would use in a fight. It was also the kind of knife that some called a boot knife, and the men that used them were without a doubt very bad men. Wil had seen a foreman run a logger out of camp for carrying one into the cook shack. But that was a long time ago and Wil couldn't remember the face.

He got back into the canoe and paddled the rest of the way home. The trip of only a few miles each way had turned out to be quite a long and perilous journey. He neared his cabin and his wife came down to the river bank to greet him. Wil was soiled and bleeding from under his hat.

"Wil! What happened to you?"

"We got some bad trouble Ma. The Andersons got burned out and all that's left of their family is Sam and Missy. The rest are dead. It looks like it was murder."

"Here Wil. Let me help you to the house. You look a little worse for wear."

Wil and Ma walked up the hill to the cabin, talking all the way. There was a lot to say about the day and they talked well into the night. They concluded that Wil better get in touch with the law up in International Falls, the closest there was in these parts. Then they came to the subject of the children. There wasn't room here, but neither of them would let a stranger have them. It was decided then that the children would come and live with them. All that it meant was that they would have to add on to the cabin and put another potato in the stew for supper. Wil told Ma about the girl Missy and how she wouldn't talk. She figured that it might come back in time. The kids were of an age where they could pretty much take care of themselves. Sam was thirteen and Missy was twelve. Ma felt that they were awful young to have to start over again. Wil's final words for the evening were that he would paddle back down to the General Store and tell Milo and Ann about their decision.

The next day, Wil put the canoe in the water and paddled again down to the store.

He walked in and told Milo about the decision to take the kids to come and live with them.

As they stood there, Sam walked in and saw Wil talking with Milo.

"Hi Sam. Are you feeling a bit better today?" asked Wil.

"Yup. But these burns on my hands are a bit tender yet."

"Do you think you can paddle a canoe?" asked Wil.

"Sure. What do you have in mind?"

"Well Sam, Ma and I had a long talk last night and we want to know if you kids would like to come live with us. We'll treat you so many ways that you're bound to like some of them." and they all laughed a little.

"I'll go tell Missy. She'll be pretty happy about that."

When he had left the store, Milo went and patted Wil on the back, telling him what a nice thing it was for them to take in the orphans.

The kids got all they needed from the store, including some new clothes and school supplies and started the trip back up river, to a new home and a new life.

Wil and Sam paddled hard upstream against the current and as they came by the burned out cabin, Missy started to cry. Silent tears flowed down her cheeks and wet her new shirt. Sam, too, had a hard time containing all of his saved up tears. As Wil paddled, he saw Sam hang his head low and cry silently. A milk cow said hello from the river bank and tried to follow Sam upstream, splashing in the shallow water. Then the other one came from over the hill and followed. As they paddled along, Sam kept shouting encouragement to the cows and by the time they got to Wil's cabin the two cows were right behind them. Sam put a halter on them and led them to the barn.

Ma came outside and welcomed them to their new home. Little Missy was sure glad to see a woman and stayed close to her, not letting her out of sight.

The next few days were spent getting to know each other. A couple of men from town had gone out to the Anderson's and got the draft team back to Wil's place. They figured to sell them because there was no need for a second team on one farm. Sam, however, changed Wil's mind when he said that he could use them to make some cash money putting up wood on his days off from school. And Wil also thought that he needed to be around things that were familiar to him. He knew how to handle the animals quite well and Wil felt comfortable after watching him talk to the team.

Inside, Ma and Missy had gotten things into somewhat of a routine. They made bread together, cooked meals together, got water together and even washed the kitchen dishes together. There was getting to be a lot more smiling and each time that Missy got close to saying something, she would withdraw and a cloud would cover her gentle spirit. Ma knew that in time she would regain her voice, but she wasn't sure how long it might take.

Life had also been difficult for Wil and Ma. They had been farming in southern Minnesota and lost a pair of twin boys in a farming accident. Then they moved back up here on the river and took a turn at farming. It was a hard life for them both and to put food on the table, they had to work from sunrise to sunset. Little Missy had taken some of the load from Ma's shoulders and it was greatly appreciated.

Within the next four weeks, there was a new addition built on the house. It was a fairly large room for the two kids and for privacy, Ma had hung a blanket down the middle of the room. Wil built each kid a straw bed and they were very satisfied with them. The two were settling in quite well.

School was getting to be a routine and even though Missy couldn't talk, she did all of her work quite well. Sam was trying hard to get good grades, but his mind always wandered to the parts of the forest where the hunting was best. Wil tried to help him, but his own education came mostly from the woods and waters of this country. He could do numbers, but some of it was still a puzzle.

It was getting on into the middle of October and Wil decided to see if young Sam had any interest in hunting. The ducks had started to come down from the north and were plentiful on the river. Saturday morning before light, Wil loaded up the canoe with decoys and shotguns and asked Sam if he wanted to go along. He looked up at Wil with a grin. Then Wil noticed that he was already dressed and waiting to be asked. He put on his coat and hat and was out the door and waiting by the canoe for Wil. They paddled up toward Hay creek and set the decoys up near a beaver lodge.

The first rays of daylight were making their way to the tops of the birch trees and Sam could hear the ducks coming from everywhere. It was still too dark to shoot, but the ducks were landing in the decoys already. Then Wil motioned to Sam to take one that was coming in right at them. The boy raised the gun, aimed and squeezed the trigger, but the duck kept flying. He did, however, manage to wake all of the mallards that had set down in the decoys. The whole sky came to life and Sam had a hard time deciding which target to shoot at. Wil never even fired his gun. He was laughing hard, watching Sam have the time of his life. He must have shot half a box of shells before he finally killed a duck. When the first one splashed into the water, Wil let out a whoop, and so did Sam. That seemed to settle Sam down some and he was able to hit at least every tenth one he tried for. Wil had knocked down six and Sam had taken two by the time that the ducks slowed down and quit flying. It had been a good hunt. Sam was careful with the gun and handled it with care, something that Wil always insisted on.

The sun was getting higher in the sky, so Wil decided it was time to head home and get some breakfast. Wil paddled and Sam picked up the decoys and their prize mallards. They both had done well and Wil was pleased with Sam's performance. The trip home proved to be a time for Sam to open up a bit. He thanked Wil for taking him along.

"You know Wil, I'm going to find who killed my folks and Sister. It might take a while, but I am going to find him."

"I know how you're feeling Sam, but you have to be careful. He's probably a really bad one. I found his knife near your house and it has the initials B.S. carved in the handle. It's sitting on the mantle back at the cabin."

"That's not much to go on. He's got your gun, too."

"Yup. And another thing is that I figure he's a logger by the boots he wore. The Sheriff says that there wasn't enough to go on either."

They paddled along with Sam getting a bit more quiet.

In Sam's mind, it was a matter of time until he would catch up with the coward that killed his family. He held a lot of hatred inside, but not to the point that it ruled his life. He was determined to find him even if it took him years to do so.

Young Missy still wouldn't or couldn't talk even though Ma tried hard to get her to speak. Each time she got near to talking, she would start sobbing. She held something dark and deep inside her and couldn't let it out yet. Ma figured that some day she would burst forth with a lot of stored up words, things that she had wanted to say for a long time. She was a beautiful young lady and extremely polite.

That winter found the family in a battle with the elements. The snow had started slowly and gained in intensity as it progressed. By the middle of December, the snow was nearly five feet deep in places.

Sam hitched up his team and cleared a path around the yard and to the barn. Then he would head off down the road plowing snow to the main road. They needed a good path to get to school and also to the General Store a few miles away. The temperatures held at thirty below at night for nearly a week and it sure used up a lot of wood. Sam had been trying to make a little money cutting firewood, but he had little time for it. His jobs around the cabin took a lot of time. On weekends, he would head into the hardwoods and cut a load to sell in town. Then he would take the money he earned and put it in the sugar bowl like Wil did. It gave him a sense of family to know that he was helping.

Christmas time was getting closer and Ma asked if they had picked out a tree yet. The kids eyes lit up with the thought of a gift and special treats that went with the season. Next Saturday morning found Wil, Sam and Missy out snowshoeing in the woods trying to find the perfect tree. It was a very cold morning and Wil figured that it was way below zero. Sam spotted one and decided that it was perfect.

He bent to clear a spot to chop it down and turned to see where Missy was so he wouldn't hit her with the axe. She was standing near Wil, jerking on his sleeve. She pointed over to his left and then ran through the snow to stand beside a six-foot-tall, perfect Christmas tree. He told Sam to hold up for a minute and they walked over to look at the tree. It was absolutely perfect, just what they had been looking for. Missy grinned from ear to ear and stood back as Sam cut it down. They were both excited as they dragged it home and into the shed to make a stand for it. Wil did the carpentry work as he always had done. It was only three days until Christmas and it wouldn't dry out too bad in that time. They knocked on the door and Ma came out to give it her smile of approval. Then they brought it into the house to thaw out for a while.

Chores were done this day in the usual manner and when lunch time arrived they all sat at the table discussing how to decorate the tree. Sam said that he knew how to make paper stars and that Missy knew how to make paper chains. She nodded her head in agreement. Ma said that she could make some popcorn to string with cranberries for more decorations. Wil contributed the candle holders for the tree and that made for an exciting afternoon. The kids were intent on putting as much on the tree as it would hold. Missy was so busy making paper chains that she lost track of what she was doing and before Ma could get her stopped, she had produced many yards of chain. They would find room for it all somehow. Ma's job was to put it all on the tree so it would look it's best. It took her a long time and a lot of smiles before it was finished.

The next Sunday found them in church singing songs of the season and listening to a sermon by a traveling preacher. The lady that played the pump organ made beautiful music as long as the kid at the bellows didn't fall asleep. They all listened intently and then it was off to the church basement for a pot luck dinner, one of the communities most enjoyed activities. There was an extreme amount of food and everyone ate a good meal. This was one occasion that even some of the local lumberjacks came to from the big timber camps.

After the meal, one of the loggers by the name of Buster Hines came and asked Wil if he could come outside to talk for a bit. They put on their jackets and stepped out into the snow. They found a spot out of the wind around the corner of the church.

"I heard that the Anderson's got burned out." said Buster.

"Yup." said Wil. "He almost got me too. He hit me over the head and took my Colt pistol and my money."

"Any idea who done it?"

"Nope. All I know is that his initials are B.S. and he probably is a lumberjack. I found his boot knife in the ashes, unburned. He wears hobnailed boots, too."

"We'll keep an eye out for him Wil. We don't need any people like that around here."

Wil thanked Buster and the two went back inside the church where it was a lot warmer. He knew that Buster would spread the word around the camps.

# CHAPTER 3
## CHRISTMAS ON THE RIVER

The morning of Christmas Eve was filled with excitement for all four of the family. There was a lot of baking to do and Missy was getting to be a real help with anything that involved food. She could make a cake that everyone loved and the small cabin smelled of Christmas goodies. There was first the scent of cinnamon and apple cider. That was one of Wil's favorite things from his time as a child. Then there was the odor of fresh vanilla. That meant that there would be a white cake for them all. There was Sam's favorite too, the smell of fresh bread. Missy loved it all and by the smiles on her face, she was doing all of the things she loved most. She would have the occasional times where a shadow of the past would cross her brow, but in general she was a wonderful and loving child. Wil had a soft spot in his old weathered heart for this little one and gave her a hug each time she came in from school.

This Christmas was going to be special for them all. There was a little money that the family had saved in the sugar bowl so Ma and Wil made a trip to the General Store for gifts. Wil hitched up the team and the small cutter. It was very cold again this day and a buffalo robe was brought out to help stay warm. The kids were given chores to do while they were gone, with instructions not to eat all of the cookies and candy. They all laughed. Wil pulled the cutter up to the door and Ma came out dressed in her warmest coat and mittens. The team turned and headed down the road, the bells tinkling sharply in the cold winter air. Wil looked over at Ma and was pleased to see such a broad smile on her face. In a short while, they pulled up to the General Store and tied the team up to the rail. When they came into the store, they were greeted warmly by Milo and Ann. There were several customers in the store and each was a friend and neighbor. Each person in turn came to say hello and wish Christmas greetings. Ma started to make her way around the store, trying to find a gift for the kids that they could afford and one that they would like. It took some time, but she found a matching scarf and mittens for Missy, a jackknife for Sam and when Wil wasn't looking, she picked up the .45 Colt that she had ordered for Wil. This was going to be a great Christmas for them all. Then she got a few groceries, items she needed for the big Christmas day meal.

She paid for all of her things with cash and went out to the cutter to wait for Wil. He saw her leave and right away went over to Milo and asked if he had gotten the new treadle sewing machine in yet. She had always done her sewing with a needle and thread by hand. Milo smiled and said that he would deliver it on Christmas morning at around 6:00, just as they said. Wil would make payments on it for 6 months as agreed. He was not one to use credit, but with Milo, it was more like a deal between friends.

The trip home had Ma a bit puzzled. He thought that Wil would have bought her something. Then it dawned on her that maybe he had made her something special, something made by his own hands.

When they came into the yard, there was Missy sitting on top of Sam, washing his face with snow. They had been in a great snowball fight and by the looks of things, Missy was winning. They jumped up when they saw the cutter coming.

"Now get back you kids." she said. "There are things in these packages that you don't need to see yet." She laughed hard and headed for the house with her packages hidden from everyone.

It was starting to get a little darker so they all went inside for some supper. Then it was time for Wil to light the tree. There were candle holders that he had made years ago and each was clipped to the branches of the Christmas tree. Carefully, he lit the candles and then Ma blew out the lanterns. The sight was, to the children, absolutely overwhelming. The tree shimmered and sparkled beautifully. The little paper stars spun in circles and Wil in his gravely old voice started to sing "Away in the Manger". The rest of the family joined in, and for a time, all that mattered was what was here in this little snow-covered cabin on the Bigfork River.

Early the next morning, Wil had gotten up to throw a few more pieces of wood on the fire. As the flames grew and danced in the hearth, he was drawn back to a time when his twin boys were still with them.

They were a pure joy to him and they were always excited about one thing or another. Christmas was a time for them to really get fired up. On one occasion, an early riser had gotten up before Wil and Ma and opened all the presents. When they got up later on Christmas morning, they saw the whole mess with wrapping paper scattered everywhere. Not knowing who had done it, they just re-wrapped all the gifts and pretended that it never happened. When they got up, the culprit saw that everything was back the same way as it was and jumped up on Wil's lap and snuggled in. There wasn't the normal excitement and he knew who had done it. So Wil passed out the gifts as usual but left his until last. When it was his turn, he looked up at Wil with big tears in his eyes and said, "I sorry Papa.".

In all the years since that happened, Wil never forgot that tender-hearted moment. He sat there this night remembering. The flames in the hearth had gone down some and the moonlight flooded the room with a soft melancholy glow through the window. Deep inside, Wil knew that his boys were in a better place.

The next morning found the children waiting quietly in their room. They were dressed and waiting for Wil and Ma to wake up. They each had peeked out at the Christmas tree and saw the presents wrapped up in brightly colored paper. Sam counted three of them and that meant that someone didn't get a gift. It perplexed him greatly.

How could there have been someone that didn't get a gift? Missy heard Wil and Ma talking and put her finger to her lips to quiet Sam. Then Wil and Ma came out smiling broadly. They knew that the children would be waiting for them so that they could open their gifts. Wil pulled out his pocket watch and saw that it was five minutes until Milo would arrive. He started a pot of coffee going on the stove and turned to see each of the family watching him, waiting for him to say it was time to open their gifts. The coffee was boiling and Wil pulled out his watch again as if something was going to happen at a certain time. They were all puzzled.

Then it was time to open the gifts. Ma was first to take a gift from under the tree and hand it to Sam. He made such a fuss over the knife. It had three blades and each was very sharp. He had never owned a knife before and it was almost like a rite of passage to him. He went first to Ma and hugged her. Then he went to Wil and thanked him with a hug. Then he went to Missy and hugged her too. He was very proud of his new knife.

Then it was time for Wil to pick a gift from under the tree and hand it to Missy. She accepted it and slowly proceeded to open it. Her eyes sparkled in the firelight of the hearth. It appeared that tears were starting and she wiped them away with the back of her hand. She pulled out the new mittens and then the scarf. They were made out of brightly colored red wool and would keep her warm even on the coldest Minnesota mornings. She first went to Ma and hugged her, giving her a kiss on the cheek. Then it was off to Wil. He got the same treatment. Then she went to her only brother and hugged him fiercely. She looked him straight in the eye and said all the things she had held inside for so long, only the sounds didn't come out. Tears ran down her cheeks and each person in the room felt themselves choking up a bit.

Then Ma went to the tree and got the package for Wil. He accepted it from her with a broad smile. As he opened it, he looked around at the rest of his family. They were all staring at him with big smiles on their faces. He pulled out the box and noticed the name Colt on the package. This hurried him up some and when he opened the box, there was a Colt revolver like the one he had carried for years before the murderer stole it from him. He thanked Ma and held it up to test the feel of it. It was exactly like the one he had lost. He had an extra holster and it fit well. He thanked his family for the fine gift and sat there admiring it.

Then it was Ma's turn, but there was one problem, it had not arrived yet. He started to say something to explain the lack of a gift when he heard sleigh bells jingling outdoors. The knock on the door followed immediately. Ma answered the door, and there stood Milo with a big grin on his face.

"Special delivery for you Ma'am. Where would you like me to place the cargo for you?"

"Well, what in the world is it?" she asked.

"Don't exactly know Ma'am, but if your husband will give me a hand, we could bring it into the house for you." said Milo, trying to look very formal.

With that the two men walked outside and brought in a large package covered with a shipping blanket. They sat it in the middle of the floor and Milo wished everyone a Merry Christmas and walked out into the morning cold.

Ma walked over to it and took off the blanket that covered it. Her eyes lit up like a birthday cake filled with candles. She saw the name Singer on the side and knew right away what she had gotten. She lifted the top and up popped the machine. She grabbed a chair and sat down to it, looking and touching it. Every once in a while she would look at Wil and smile. Then she jumped up and ran to Wil hugging him around the neck.

"Never in my life have I had a gift like this. Thank you Wil Morgan."

And such was their Christmas. They all ate too much and laughed a lot too. It was far nicer than they had even hoped for. Wil went outside to shoot his new Colt and Ma stayed inside learning how to use her new Singer sewing machine. The kids played in the snow and together they did all the chores, giving each animal some extra oats or hay as is the custom on Christmas.

The days lengthened and the winter snow clouds gave way to the puffy clouds of spring. Snow melted at a furious rate and ran into the Bigfork River making for some loud nights as the water cascaded toward Hudson Bay. People talked about things like gardens and such and what new kind of seed was available.

Sam walked back to his old home on the river one spring day. It was quite a distance, but he was a strong young man and Wil had confidence in him. As he neared the old place, he started to feel all of the old feelings he had the day his family was killed. He remembered the fire, and the way Missy and him huddled together to keep warm, not knowing what they should do. He remembered his mother's screams from inside the burning house.

He found a chunk of firewood and sat down staring at the now cold pile of ashes. Some were wood ashes and some the remains of his Mother, Father and little baby Sister. It was pretty hard on a young man to come to grips with something so bad. He knew that some day he would find the man that killed them and was ready even at such a young age to take care of the problem. He got up and looked around the old homestead. He found his old slingshot and gave it a toss into the ashes. Then he found Missy's doll, much worse for wear after spending the winter under the snow piles. The whole scene seemed nearly dreamlike to him. His thoughts of times past left questions in his mind as to whether they were real or from his many hours of trying to remember things from days long ago. He did, however, have a clear picture in his mind of his mother and father's faces. The little sister was starting to fade and that bothered him badly. This was his only way to keep them alive.

He walked down by the river and looked around to see if anything had changed. It was still the same and would forever be the same. Nothing changed about the river. He looked up stream and saw someone coming in a canoe. As it got closer, Sam saw a man paddling that he hadn't seen before. He was a big man with black greasy hair. He paddled in toward Sam and grabbed hold of a small tree to steady the canoe.

"Are you lost boy?"

"Nope. I'm just looking around."

"You used to live here?"

"Yup, a long time ago."

Sam saw that the man was carrying a sidearm.

"You want a ride down river?"

"Nope."

Sam looked the man in the eye, steadily, without blinking. He thought for a second about the gun and feared some for his safety. With that the man let go of the small tree and paddled out into the current. Sam sat down and thought about what had happened. The man carried a gun, but so did a lot of men. Sam was suspicious, but he wasn't sure of what. He turned to go back up hill to head home. He walked into the woods following a deer trail that led along the river. In an hour or so he was back home walking into the cabin. Ma greeted him and asked if he wanted some coffee and a cookie. Sam sat for a while thinking about the man on the river.

One of Sam's friends came over to talk to him that afternoon. He wanted to see if Sam could go fishing down by the rapids. The Walleyes were biting good and there were some big ones being caught. Off they went with Ma's approval and instructions to be extra careful. They dug some worms and headed down the road to the rapids. The fishing was great and the boys caught several nice fish. There were a lot of people there from town, all taking advantage of what the river could provide. Sam was standing on a log that aimed out into the white water. The current hit hard on the log, sending occasional plumes of spray high into the air. Everyone was intent on what they were doing and Sam didn't notice the man with the greasy hair walk up to the log he was standing on. The man looked around and when nobody was looking in his direction, he rolled the log , sending Sam into the rapids, headed downstream at a very fast rate. Everyone yelled at the same time and all eyes were on Sam's dilemma. No one looked to see what had caused the accident and the big man slipped off into the woods leaving the commotion behind him.

The cold water hit Sam like a hammer and he knew right away that he was in trouble. He came to the surface downstream from

27

everyone else and new that if he were to live, he had to save himself. He looked to see where he was and swam to the nearest point of dry ground. As he got near it, he was swept once again past it and downstream. He was getting weak and thought that his next try might be his last. Instead of swimming toward the place he wanted to go, he tried to get to where the current would sweep him by close to it. He had little strength left and used every bit he had to save himself. He felt the ground under his chest and scrambled out onto the bank. He was shaking hard but he didn't know if it was from fear, cold or anger. He didn't see who moved his log, but he knew that it didn't move by itself.

Soon, Milo and a friend ran up to him and wrapped him with a coat. He was still shaking as they pushed him up the hill and into the store. Ann saw all the commotion and had laid a blanket on the stove to warm it. She sent him into the bedroom to take all of his clothes off and wrap up in the blanket. When he came outside, there were questions coming from everywhere. He didn't know what had happened or who moved the log. He heard a noise and in walked Wil, looking for Sam.

"What happened Sam?" asked Wil.

"I'm not sure, but I think someone tried to kill me."

The whole room went silent. Ma walked in and grabbed him, holding him close. She had a lot of tears saved up and she let them go all at once.

Later, after things calmed down some back home, he and Wil sat in the kitchen and by the light of a kerosene lamp, discussed the whole day. Sam told Wil of the man in the canoe and the gun he had. He didn't leave anything out and told the whole story. Wil figured that the man had come to kill him after Sam saw his face back on the river. These were hard things to think of for a young man but he was growing up fast, whether he wanted to or not. Missy sat by him and listened.

Summer came, and with it hordes of mosquitoes. Anyone that went outside after dark lost a lot of blood to those creatures of the night. Even a trip to the outhouse was a hazardous one due to those swarming hordes. Then in the latter part of June, the temperatures dropped below freezing for one night. All of the mosquitoes died and nobody missed them much. There was, however, a lot of loss in the neighboring gardens. All of the new tomato plants got killed and it set back the potatoes severely. Everyone wondered if there would even be a vegetable crop, but in time, everything came back and the remainder of the summer was enjoyed without so many mosquitoes.

July brought the big Fourth celebration and the kids all had a good time. There were sparklers and small firecrackers. In the evening, the sky lit up over the river with loud bangs and sparkling colors. Then a big pot-luck dinner capped off the evening for everyone. These were good times for the community.

October brought harvest, and there was a lot to do for everyone. There was hay to be cut and potatoes to be dug and put away for the winter. There was also an abundance of squash to be stored. There was the butchering to be done and with Sam's extra hands to help, the job went smoothly. Ma cut and canned as much pork as she could handle. It was starting to look like it would be an easier winter than they had for some time. When Wil butchered a steer, he sold half at the General Store and that brought cash money to buy the things that they needed for the kids.

Wil turned 40 in October and Ma baked him a large birthday cake. They sang Happy Birthday to him and that made him feel good. Then after the cake, he looked around to see what Ma had gotten him for a present. He didn't say anything, not wanting to hurt anyone's feelings. She always got him some sort of gift. Sometimes it was a new pair of homemade socks or maybe a shirt, but today he looked shyly around and saw nothing at all. The look on his face gave him away and Ma finally came up and sat on his lap. She was still the prettiest woman he had ever seen.

"Are you ready for your present?"

"Why sure!" he said with a laugh.

Ma put her arms around Wil's neck, kissed him on the cheek and whispered something into his ear.

"We're going to have a baby."

Wil had a hard time with this one. He had hurt his ears when some dynamite had exploded too close to him and he thought that they might be wearing out.

"What did you say?"

"We're going to have a baby."

This time he caught what she said and erupted with a howl that could have been heard all the way to Hudson Bay. He got up quickly and almost dropped his wife right on the floor. He grabbed her by the arm and danced her around the room to the sound of Sam laughing. Missy stood there grinning.

"Oh Ma. That's wonderful. I thought that I was too old to have a new baby."

Ma said. "You're too old? What about me?"

The house was filled with laughter and smiles. The kids were now fifteen and sixteen and by the time the new baby would need a room, they would be all grown.

# CHAPTER 4
## THE LOGGING CAMPS

Buster Hines walked into the yard one frosty morning early and asked Wil if he had some time to talk for a bit. The two men walked down by the river and sat on Wil's favorite log bench, the place where serious conversations took place. Buster asked if he had heard anything about the Jack that killed the Andersons. Wil said that he hadn't heard anything that he could sink his teeth into but he was still looking.

Buster commenced to tell what he had heard so far, and it made Wil's eyes grow dark with anger. Buster had been a lumberjack for a long time and had gotten to know a lot of men in the northern part of the state. It seemed that last winter, Les Anderson had been working for the Gut and Liver Camp further north on the Bigfork River. Les was a hard worker and like a lot of family men, he saved every cent that he earned for his family. None of the logging camps allowed the men to gamble, but on one night in the bunkhouse, a few of the men started a poker game. There was a little guy that everyone called Marty, a saw filer by the name of Carl, the blacksmith Lou and a big man that nobody liked, called Scooter. By the light of a couple of kerosene lamps, the game got going in earnest. It was thought that Jacks never had much money, but some had been saving for quite some time. The table was an upturned cracker crate with a wool blanket for a table top.

The game had been growing in size for a couple of hours and Lou had dropped out when his losses totaled $5.00. That was a big sum of money to him. That left Carl, Marty and Scooter. Les sat on his bunk in the shadows watching the game, not saying anything. None of it was his business, anyway. He saw that Carl and Scooter were ganging up on Marty, using a subtle nod when either had a good hand. They would bet and raise until the pot was large, then they would swoop in for the kill. Les kept quiet watching the poor man get cleaned out. Then something caught his eye. Scooter had palmed an ace and put it inside his shirt. Marty was sweating hard, and had lost nearly all of the money he had been saving for his family. The betting was getting hot and heavy and Marty must have had a good hand because he kept raising. Then it was time for show and tell. Les saw Scooter switch his hidden card and stand up to take the pot.

Les jumped up from his bunk and ripped open Scooter's shirt letting the card fall to the floor. Then the fight was on for sure. Scooter bent over, pulling a knife from his boot and swung at Les. Then Les dodged and hit the big man solidly behind the ear and that was the end of the fight. In a few minutes the foreman was there, and had a few words with the men. No more gambling – and as for Scooter, he got run out of another camp along with his partner Carl. The loggers took all of the money and gave it back to the ones that had lost, but on this evening in the woods, there was a fierce enemy made that swore vengeance. Scooter had blood in his eye and his anger was directed at Les Anderson. Les could take care of himself in any situation, but he would have to be extra careful for a while.

Wil's eyes narrowed and he just sat and thought for a spell.

"Do you have any idea what Scooter's real name was?" asked Wil.

"I found out a couple weeks ago. It's Brad Sherman. I think he's from up around Atikokan in Canada. He's wanted up there by the Mounties I heard."

Wil went into the house and came back in a couple of minutes with the knife he had found at the Anderson place. Carved into the handle were the initials B.S. This was proof enough for Wil, but it might be another thing altogether to find this murderer. It looked to Wil as if this guy Scooter had gotten his revenge by throwing a kerosene lantern through the window of Les's cabin and in the process, had killed his wife and daughter as well. This was a bad man and the world would be a better place without him.

Wil looked up and saw Sam walking toward them. He had to know all of what Wil had heard. There were tears forming in Sam's eyes, but his anger wouldn't let them flow. Now he wanted revenge for the death of his family. The pieces of the puzzle were starting to come together. Sam now knew what the man looked like and that was why he dumped him in the river. He wanted to be rid of the rest of the family and now Sam feared for Missy, too.

Wil asked Buster to stay for dinner and that suited him well. Ma had a reputation as a great cook and Buster could eat a fair bit if the opportunity presented itself. He'd stay, but this afternoon there was work that needed to be done and Buster's extra hands would help a lot. Wil had to put up about four more cords of firewood and Buster sure knew his end of a two-man saw. They hitched up the dray and headed into the woodlot where the best firewood was. They started by cutting down some big ash trees and then commenced to limbing them. Sam had a new double-bit axe and knew how to use it pretty well. Buster commented to Wil that the boy would make a pretty good logger some day.

After Sam finished the limbing, Buster and Wil took to cutting it up in chunks for the stove. Then Sam came behind them and split it in pieces, small enough to go into the stove. Then he threw it up on the dray to be hauled to the house. In about four hours time, the four cords were all cut down, but only about one was split and hauled. Wil still figured that this was a good amount of firewood, anyway.

Ma poked her head out the door and yelled for the men to come to supper.

"Wash up good or ya don't get fed." she laughed.

The men came in and the first thing they noticed was a huge

platter full of fried chicken. This had to be Buster's all time favorite and his eyes lit up brightly. Missy sat by Buster, but eventually had to move over a bit to keep from getting hit with his boarding house reach. His manners weren't the best, but he was used to working in the camps and you ate fast and got your share or you went without. Ma had made boiled potatoes and gravy, corn and biscuits. Buster figured that he had hit the mother lode for sure. Even Wil was surprised to see how much he could pack away. Then in a short while, he belched and pushed himself back from the table. The others were still eating when he walked out the door for a smoke. He didn't say a word, and when Wil came outside, Buster was back in the woods splitting wood again. He figured that he had to pay them back for the fine meal.

"Does your missus always cook like that?" asked Buster.

"No. Sometimes we eat better." said Wil laughing.

Buster was laughing hard and almost hit his foot with the axe. The two men had been good friends for several years.

They worked hard until it got dark and walked slowly back to the cabin. Wil thanked Buster for everything and invited him to come back any time he came into town. He also told him that Ma's cooking got better every day, so he shouldn't stay gone too long.

A few weeks later, Wil had another visitor knock on his door. It was the Sheriff from Koochiching County, Bill Dawson.

"Come in Bill." Wil said.

"Got some bad news Wil. Buster Hines got killed, and it looks like it was with a knife."

Wil was a bit surprised because Buster was a tough man and he didn't think that he could be taken by anyone.

"Do you have any idea who did it?"

"Nope. We saw some tracks, but that was all."

"What kind of tracks?"

"Looked like hobnail boots, but most of the jacks wear them."

Wil mulled it over in his head a while.

"Bill, I got a bad feeling that it was the same one who killed the Andersons."

Then Wil related to the sheriff about what Buster had told him. The sheriff said that Buster had been asking questions around the camp. The other jacks knew that Buster didn't have any family but was close friends with Wil and Ma. The killer had come up behind him while he was hitching up a team of horses and stuck a knife in his heart from behind. The other loggers found him that evening, dead. He had lost another long time friend and now he was mad. Wil asked if a jack by the name of Brad Sherman was working at any camps in the area. It wasn't a name that the sheriff had heard, but he'd keep his eyes open. Wil proceeded to tell the lawman all that he knew from Buster and that was enough for the Sheriff to go looking for someone. Up to that point, he had no solid clues as to even which direction to look. Now he had a name, but no face. A man could change his name and blend in with the other jacks at any camp. Sam listened closely and kept all he heard deep inside. Some day he would take care of this man himself. He wasn't going to go on a hunt for him, but he knew in time, they would meet. Then he would do whatever needed to be done.

The last of the firewood had no more than been put away than winter hit another hard blow with a fierceness that they hadn't seen for quite some time. For November, it was unusual to see temperatures of thirty below zero. From inside the cabin, you had to scrape a hole in the frost to see out of the windows. That always meant severe cold.

The morning trips to school were getting to be hard on the kids too, so Wil hitched up the small cutter every morning and took them there. It seemed that the horse liked to have something to do, too. He would prance prettily until it started to feel like work. It wasn't the cold that bothered the kids so much, but the wind cut through even their heaviest coats. The trips home were usually when the air had warmed some, but it didn't happen this year. The cold came and stayed.

One day in early November, Wil went out to get some water and the cistern pump was frozen up solid. They melted snow on the

Monarch wood range to boiling and poured it into the pump. All the water in the world was no good to them if they couldn't get it out of the ground. This required several buckets of hot water and finally after a couple of hours of trying, the old pump gave up some of it's precious water. This was a normal ritual at least several times throughout the winter, but it usually didn't start so early.

Wil was starting to notice that the deer were hanging around the barn more than usual. They were having a tough time too, and the wolves chased them constantly in the deep snow. When this amount of snow came so early, it meant that the deer would starve in huge numbers. It took all of their energy to get around to find browse in the deep snow. Their gradual weakening meant that the wolves ate good, at least until the deer were all gone. Then they would start on Wil's livestock.

Wil knew the result of the deep snow and decided to take some venison for Ma to can. It wasn't like going hunting. It was like slaughtering his farm animals. One night at the dinner table, Wil winked at Ma and then asked Sam if he would mind shooting a deer for them on Saturday. His grin showed how he felt about the family having confidence in him. His heart was swelling with pride and all that came from his lips was, "Sure." Inside, he felt himself growing to be a man, with a man's responsibilities.

Saturday morning found Sam all dressed in his warmest clothes with the 12-gauge slung over his shoulder. He had some buckshot in the chamber and off he went. He walked around the back side of the barn and out to where the deer had been yarding. His trip was one of only about 200 yards and Wil heard the shotgun go off. Not too long later there was another shot, then another. Wil looked at Ma and knew that something was wrong. Then he heard three more shots quite close together. Wil put on his Colt and grabbed the old 45-70 Government rifle and headed out the door fast. Another shot went off by the barn and he took off running as fast as he could. What greeted him was a young man with the gun to his shoulder getting ready to fire another shot. Wil looked to where he was aiming and saw four wolves crouched down low coming right toward Sam. He took out the Colt and started to fire at them. The combination of two men and three guns took care of the wolf problem in short order. Wil looked at Sam and the boy melted in tears. Sam had faced a serious threat to his life and hadn't backed down from it. He had shot a deer and then the wolves came and tried to take it. He shot one and then they came for him. He kept shooting, but was scared and wasn't hitting the way he normally would have. All told between the two men, they had killed six wolves and one deer. The bounty money on the wolves was $3.00 each and that was money that they needed. The deer would be canned and enjoyed for weeks.

Missy was growing into a pretty young lady and the new skills that she learned from Ma made her proud. She had been sewing on a new dress for church and each time that something wasn't done quite right, she would tear it out and start again. She was in her own way a perfectionist and that pleased Ma greatly. The winter kept them inside a lot and that brought out her talents.

Ma had been having some trouble with her lungs and she kept everyone at bay by telling them that it was nothing. One Sunday morning, Wil got up and made his usual pot of coffee pouring a cup for each of them. Ma's coffee got cold before she got to it. In a short while, Wil went in to kid her about sleeping in late like the rich folks. As soon as he saw her, he knew that something was wrong, dreadfully wrong.

He walked over to her and she was staring at the ceiling and breathing hard. Wil put his hand on her forehead and knew that this was trouble. He went out in the kitchen and called Sam to go to the General Store and send a message to get a doctor here as soon as he could. In a very few minutes, they heard Sam outside with the horse. Then he was gone.

Wil walked back into the bedroom and put a cold wet cloth on Ma's forehead. She was having a hard time breathing and her lungs wheezed with each breath. Her hands were at her sides and she looked like she was afraid to move. In the very best of circumstances, the doctor wouldn't be here for several hours.

"What do you want me to do Ma? Ma! What should I do?"

She whispered softly and Wil couldn't make out what she said. She tried again and sunk back on the pillow, tired from her effort. Wil looked around the kitchen and saw a jar of Menthol and right next to it was some wild sassafras. He got a big pot of water boiling on the stove and then proceeded to make a blanket tent over the top of Ma's head. When the water was good and hot he put in a big scoop of menthol and some sassafras. The resulting cloud of steam surrounded Ma's face and she tried hard to breathe deeply. Being four months pregnant was scary for her, too. She was very frightened that she would lose the baby if she got much worse.

There was a knock on the door and Ann Miskovich from the store walked right into their bedroom. She took off the tent blanket and felt Ma's wrist, checking her pulse.

"Now Wil, you gotta get under that blanket with her and help her breathe. It looks a lot like she got the 'monya'. Keep her spirits up and help her breathe. Then try to get her to take a deep breath once in a while."

Wil did as he was told but it looked like Ma was getting weaker. He went to the kitchen for some more hot water and when he was alone, he felt tears of deep sadness flood over him. He knew how bad it looked, and asked God if he would spare this lady. Wil wasn't a praying man, but on this day in this little cabin by the river, he poured his heart out to God. Pneumonia was almost always a killer.

Sam got back shortly and said that it would take time for the Doc to get there and to put her in a steam tent. That, all by itself, made Wil feel better. He was doing all he could. Night came and Ma kept getting weaker. Her eyes would flutter open when he spoke and toward midnight, she slept. Doc Williams came into the yard shortly after midnight and looked pretty rough himself. It had been a long ride for him but when his friend Wil called, it was time to pay back a favor or two. He looked at Ma and shook his head.

"There's not much else we can do Wil." said the Doc. "We don't have the medicine that will work for pneumonia. She only has a slight chance that she'll pull through and I can't do a thing about it."

He hung his head like a defeated man. Doc's final words were that if she could make it through Monday, she might stand a chance. He said to keep the steam tent going but most of all pray. That would do more good than anything else. He walked out into the extreme cold to leave and found that Sam had given his horse some water and oats for the trip home. He smiled at the boy and disappeared down the road in the dark.

Wil kept the steam going all night and the praying almost a continuous whisper on his lips. Morning came and with it, no improvement in Ma's condition. Her eyes fluttered once in a while when Wil tried to give her water. The routine continued through the day and at almost dark, there was another knock on the door. Missy opened it to find Wil's old friend chief Bustikogan standing there covered with frost. He came in and stood by the fireplace to take the chill off. Then he asked Sam where Wil was.

"He's in there with Ma. She's pretty sick."

He walked into the bedroom and touched the arm of his friend Wil. Then he looked under the steam tent at Ma and touched her head. Quietly he walked back out into the kitchen. Busti looked over at Missy and told her to get some more water boiling on the stove. Missy did what she was told and in very few minutes, Busti came out of the bedroom and walked to the stove. He took the pouch from around his neck and poured the contents onto the table. There were some small bones and pieces of wood shavings, but what caught Missy's eye was the piece of white chalk-like stuff. Busti looked through the items and put some of them into the pot to boil. The resultant smell nearly drove everyone from the cabin. It had a smell like something had died and rotted away. As the concoction boiled down it reduced to a heavy black syrup. Busti removed it from the heat and told Sam to set it outside for a bit to cool. Then in a few minutes, he went out and claimed his creation. He didn't come right back in so Sam went to the window and looked outside. There was their friend Chief Bustikogan chanting and walking in circles in the snow. Sam didn't know quite what to make of it. After a short while, Busti came back in and poured the stuff into a cup and went in to see Ma. He took the steam blanket from her head and held her up to drink what he had made. As she started to swallow, she gagged on the stuff but Busti remained calm and persisted with his work. Finally, he got it all down her and gave her a sip of water. She lay back on the pillow and closed her eyes. Busti and Wil came out and sat down by the fire. It was near 2:00 a.m. and they were pretty tired.

"What did you give Ma? It smelled terrible."

"Some of it was herbs and some a bit of mud from around a bubbling pool far in the north. My people use it to heal their wounds. By morning she will be better, or gone to be with the Great Spirit." said Busti. "She has a strong spirit, but her body is very weak. It may have been too late for her."

Again Wil walked outside to be alone and pray.

Morning found everyone in the cabin asleep. Wil woke with a start and ran in to see how Ma was. As he came into the bedroom, Ma opened her eyes and saw him. She smiled a bit and went back to sleep. Wil turned to leave and ran into Busti. He too was smiling.

The next few days were spent regaining her strength. She ate a lot of chicken broth and drank a lot of tea. She was on the mend and the household was thankful to Busti for his medicine. He brought her in some herbal tea but Ma politely refused. Wil thought it might be that she remembered the stuff that Busti healed her with.

The winter passed and Ma healed. The pneumonia nearly took her life but she remained strong enough that she didn't lose the baby. By Spring, she was getting pretty big and had a hard time bending over. Wil beamed each time their eyes met. He had lost his twins, and now was going to have another chance at a family. Missy helped all she could and took a load of work from Ma. Even though she still didn't talk, they communicated well. Missy was 16 now and a very pretty girl. Sam was 17 and talked of working in the big lumber camps. He kidded his sister about getting married some day.

# CHAPTER 5
## FIRST ADVENTURE

As the time approached for Ma to deliver the new family member, she kept busy knitting and making all the things that they would need for the new arrival. Wil kept her supplied with yarn of various colors and even Missy helped by learning how to knit. She spent each evening by the fire trying hard to learn new stitches. She was a very intelligent young lady and it came out each time she tried something new.

April of 1923 brought a new life into their house. A boy just over the eight pound mark took over their cabin on the river. With Missy, Sam, Ma, Wil and the new boy, they were all having some difficulty finding a place to sit at the kitchen table. Ma stayed pretty busy most of the time caring for the baby and the rest helped as much as they could. Within just a few weeks of his birth, that little lad had complete control of the family.

At dinner one evening, Sam brought up that he had heard that they were hiring men out in Montana and wondered what Wil thought of him going all that way out west. At the age of 17, Sam pretty well made all of his own decisions, but to be polite, he asked for Wil's blessing on the first adventure of his life. He was sure tough enough to handle the job, but these were some hard men that he would be working with. He would have to pull his weight with the other jacks or get run off. Sam knew that he could do it.

"You're a tough young man Sam and I sure hate to see you go. Montana is some beautiful country, and it seems that no matter which direction you walk, it's always uphill."

"Some of my other friends are going too so we kinda figured that we'd all go together. I been saving my firewood money for quite a while now and I got enough to get me started."

"You'll need to have some money with you alright, but don't flash it around. There's men that would kill you for a five spot."

"I'll keep my nose clean and do my work."

"Let's go in and have some supper." said Wil.

With that they went in and washed up for supper. Not much was said until the meal was nearly done.

"I'll be heading for Montana next week Ma. I got a good chance to get a job cutting pine in the mountains. They pay by the piece and I can make as much money as I'm willing to work. What do you think?"

"You got your schooling to think about Sam. You still have one year to get through." said Ma.

"I can't wait any more Ma. I gotta get on with my life."

Ma smiled and gave her blessing as well. Missy smiled and gave Sam a hug.

"I promise I'll write at least once a month." said Sam.

Missy had a few tears but she grinned a lot too. Wil, not prone to such sentiment walked out the door to get some fresh air.

Monday morning found Sam sitting on the steps of the General Store waiting for the others to show up. He was a couple of hours early but didn't want to miss his ride west. He always liked to sit and watch the water bouncing off the big boulders in the rapids. A freckle faced kid walked up to Sam with a small pack on his back and soon two others about his age formed the entire group of adventurers. Then at exactly 8:00 a.m. they walked over to an old truck and got settled in for a long ride. They would keep close track of how much money they spent and divide the expenses up among them. Not much was said as they slowly left the river behind them. Just as they went by the General Store, Sam let out a hellacious war whoop and they all laughed.

Montana in May of 1923 was indeed a wild place. There were few paved roads and the truck was plagued with flat tires. The trip was going smoothly except for that. They were quite a way past Miles City Montana when they got their first glimpse of mountains rising in the distance. Sam was having a hard time keeping his voice down lest he show his youthful exuberance to the others. Being grown up meant that he had to leave behind some of his childish ways.

Camp that night was made a bit early. The had their first taste of what a sunset on the mountains looked like and they were surely impressed. Night found them shivering in their blankets from the cold mountain air out of the west. Morning coffee not only tasted good, but some felt that it saved their lives. Sam grinned at the thought of seeing the mountains first hand.

Five more hours of driving got them within a short distance of the camp they were looking for. A small town gave them a chance to fill up the gas tank and get directions to the camp. Sam bought some bread and meat for sandwiches and the whole crew sat by the road eating their noon meal.

One of the boys named Ralph seemed like he was a bit nervous about asking for a job, but figured that his good looks would get him a pretty good one. They all laughed hard.

They pulled into the camp at 4:00 and there was nobody around except for in the cook shack. They walked in to ask for some information and a Chinese man with a big meat cleaver headed for them jabbering loudly and swinging the weapon around like a madman. They retreated to the outdoors and decided it might be safer to sit and wait for someone else to show up. Their first bout with the camp cook made them wonder what the other men were like.

As it was starting to get dark, one by one, small trucks and teams of horses started to come into camp. They sat and watched for a while. Soon, a tall dark man walked up to them and asked what they wanted in his camp. He was the camp foreman.

Sam was the first on his feet.

"I'm looking for a job and I heard that you were hiring."

"Now who in the hell told you that? I got all the men I need. Where you from?" he grumbled.

"We're from the Bigfork River in Minnesota." said Sam.

The foreman looked Sam straight in the eye and asked if he ever did any logging. He seemed to be somewhat impressed by where they were from.

"I been pulling my end of a saw since I was big enough to walk and so have these boys, er, I mean men. We was all raised in the big timber camps and we can handle an axe too."

The foreman looked over the rest of the crew and then said, "Hold out your hands."

They all held out the palms of their hands and the foreman looked a little less fearsome.

"Pay's by the piece. You each get your own mark and you put it on each piece you cut. Payday is the last day of the month. You can bunk in the end cabin. He pointed off north. Around here, you eat at 5 a.m. right here in the cook shack. At noon Cookie brings out some vittles by horse and wagon and then at night you stand here and wait for him to come out and blow the dinner horn. Eat fast and get the hell out of the cook shack. No talking allowed."

The foreman looked like he might have gone through this a few times before. As they stood there talking, they heard the horn blow and a small stampede of men ran past them and into the cook shack. The new men stood there watching.

"Are ya waiting for a personal dinner invitation?" asked the foreman. "You won't get one around here and you damned sure will starve. Go get in line and look me up after you're done."

Sam led the foursome into a dimly lit chow hall filled with tables and benches. Each man grabbed a large plate and the cook filled it with meat and potatoes. There was a big coffee pot on each table and each man filled his cup. As soon as they were seated, Ralph commented that the food looked pretty good. That turned out to be the wrong thing to do. Once again he had raised the ire of the little Chinaman. He was swinging a meat cleaver around Ralph's head like a man possessed. Ralph was totally confused and kept his mouth shut while the man raved.

Each table had pie enough for each place if you ate quick. The man next to Sam made a grab for his pie. Sam's hand came down over the man's wrist and the two locked eyes. Sam looked him full in the eye and slowly shook his head no. The man let loose his pie and Sam finished his meal. The others in his group kept silent and walked out the door. Soon Sam appeared and they all seemed glad to see him alive.

After they got their gear put away in the bunkhouse, they went and looked up the foreman of the camp.

"I watched that little business about your pie. Are you trying to get yourself killed or do you like to live dangerously? That's Tom Anderson, and from what I heard, he'd kill a man for far less than that."

"Then why don't you run him off?" asked Sam.

"Well, he's probably the best damned jack I ever had working for me. Good help is terrible important here. We get log contracts, and by damn if we don't fill 'em, we're out of business. I never lost a contract yet, so ya just better keep your nose clean. Understand?"

Sam and the others knew darned well what he meant. If push came to shove, Sam would be out of work and he really wanted this job.

In the morning, the boss came up to the new guys waiting in line for their breakfast.

"I'm going to put you men each with an old-timer. They'll show you the ropes."

While they were eating, the boss went up to a table and told four of the men to take Sam and his bunch for the week and show them how things were done. Right away Sam noticed that Tom Anderson was in the group. Sam never backed down from anyone and figured that if Anderson did his share of the work that he wouldn't be too tough on him. For his age, he was tough as nails and looked it too.

The days work began as soon as it was light enough to see. The first thing that Sam noticed was that the trees were a lot smaller than what he was used to and so were the saws. They were small whipsaws, no more than 5 feet long, hardly a chore for one back on the river. They would notch the tree and fall it downhill. Then they would limb it and cut the top off when it got down to 8 inches wide. The rest they left in tree lengths.

Sam looked over at Tom and told him that this was hardly a job for two men. He would run the saw and Tom could do the limbing. Tom figured that Sam was trying to get the easier job and said that he would run the saw. Sam wasn't about to argue since he was new on the job.

Both men kept up a ferocious pace and by noon, they had their mark on a serious pile of timber. Sam paused a moment to wipe the sweat from his forehead and as he turned toward Tom, he saw a tree coming at him, silent as death. He had no time to move and dropped down alongside of the one he had been working on. The tree came down right on top of him with a great whooshing sound. If he hadn't been alert, he'd have been dead.

Sam got up off the ground and looked up hill at Tom, a total fury trying hard to overtake him. He slowly walked up to Tom.

"You're getting a little close with them trees, Tom. Next time you better do the job right or you'll be spittin' teeth. Got it?"

Tom grinned broadly and that left Sam wondering if it was a mistake or not.

The rest of the day was uneventful and the two cut a lot of timber. That evening as the tallies were brought up to the foreman, he went to Sam and asked him how they put up almost twice the timber as the rest of the crews in the camp. He figured that they had padded the books.

"Well, we work smarter like my old friend Wil taught me. One man on the saw and one on the axe. These little trees don't hardly get me sweating." Sam laughed.

Well, now the light came on in the foreman's mind and he went to his shack and ordered a dozen one-man saws. The new saws came into camp the next week and the production of the camp nearly doubled. The men all made more money and so did the owners.

Back on the Bigfork River, things were getting into what some called normal. summer and the first of the harvest were beginning. Ma and Missy were putting up huge amounts of berries for the winter. Wil would look at the jars lined up and silently hope that the winter wouldn't last that long. He was used to having Sam around for haying but the boy had grown up and was on his own now. He'd write once in a while and seemed to be making a name for himself in the mountains. He worked hard and expected his partner for the day to do the same.

Missy was going into the 11th grade in school and it seemed that she was more interested in the boys than she had ever been. She didn't talk yet and that gave her some trouble but she managed to do well in school anyway.

One evening in late July someone knocked on their door at about supper time. Wil went to the door and there stood one of the young men from down the river.

"Is Missy home?" he asked.

Wil sized him up and said. "Now where in the hell do you think she'd be? Missy you got a visitor." He was truly enjoying making this young man twist in the wind.

Missy came to the door and saw her friend Peter. She smiled broadly and motioned him to come in and sit for a while.

"What's your name boy?" asked Wil.

"I'm Peter Davis. I just stopped in to see Missy for a bit."

Missy came over to him and motioned for him to sit at the table with them and have some supper. At first, he said that he had already eaten but then decided to eat anyway, since Missy had cooked the meal mostly by herself.

As he was eating, Wil grilled him mercilessly on everything from his religion to schooling to what he did for a living and then asked his age to boot. He was adept at protecting his family from outsiders. Wil wanted to know mostly where he met Missy. She was starting to feel a bit uncomfortable at the questioning and reached down and pinched Wil's leg. He jumped a bit and then grinned at her.

The meal was eaten and as the dishes were cleared, Wil asked

Peter to come outside and sit by the river with him. When they were alone, Wil resumed his interrogation.

"What do you do for a living Pete?"

"I work in the timber camps as a pencil pusher and on Sundays I fill in as a sky pilot." said Peter.

Wil's eyes popped open at that and he started to grin again. Wil also found out that they had gone to school together for a while last year and were friends. They always ate their lunch together.

Now this was starting to sound a bit better thought Wil. Sounded to him like they might make a good couple, but Peter had no such intentions. He had just stopped in to say hello to his school friend.

"I have to be back at work tomorrow so if it's alright with you, can I talk to Missy for a bit?"

Wil then realized that he had taken much of the visiting time young Peter wanted to give to Missy.

"Why sure!" said Wil. "You sit right here and I'll go get her."

In short order, Wil, Ma and Missy all came out and sat down by the river in the shade. It had been a hot day and the breeze off the river felt good to them all. Missy and Peter sat down on the grass and Wil and Ma took the bench. Conversation ran smoothly and Missy nodded her approvals and shook her head no to some things, but the smile never left her face.

Wil looked at Missy and thoughts of the fire ran through his head like a fast river. What terrible thing had she seen that took her ability to talk! Each time she looked like she was going to say something, her hands would start to quiver and the color would leave her face.

"What are you doing Sunday afternoon, Peter?" asked Ma.

"I don't have anything planned."

"Why don't you come for dinner and we can churn up a nice batch of strawberry ice cream too?"

Everyone looked at Missy and she was smiling broadly.

The summer went on and Peter spent more and more time with Missy. It appeared as if there was a serious relationship in the making.

Peter was gaining responsibility in the company he worked for and was making a bit more money which he always saved for that "rainy day". Sunday found him at the pulpit and it seemed that he had the makings for a fine preacher. Missy made the decision not to go back to school in the fall and got a job cooking at the same camp Peter worked at. She was a big hit with the men and the owner sent the old cook packing. So at the age of 18, Missy was in charge of the cook shack. She had three cookies to help her and she made meals that the men loved.

Winter logging was now in full swing with a great many men in the camp. Missy had over a hundred men to cook for and she proved that she was up to it. Once in a while, an old jack would make a comment on how pretty she was and the wrath of the other men descended on him like a cloud. They were all very protective of her and nothing off-color was ever allowed.

The morning's breakfast was no more than done when she would start on lunch. She made hundreds of sandwiches and many gallons of coffee. Then she would load the three swingdingles and the cookies would bring lunch to the men.

Just after lunch she would start some kind of meat roasting in the ovens and the cookies would start peeling potatoes. She cooked many pies and cakes for dessert and the men worked hard to keep their jobs in this camp. The word had gotten out about their cook and a lot of men showed up looking for work because of the cook.

Back in the mountains of Montana, young Sam had made a name for himself as being a tough jack with a quick smile. He always seemed happy to be working. There were no others around that could cut as much timber as him, though he was put to the test several times with small wagers.

On Saturday night he would go to town with the rest of the men from Minnesota and look around at the various saloons. His favorite was "Dirty Annie's" and the entertainment was worth a weeks pay. There was music in one form or another each payday. Sometimes it was a piano player or maybe just a man with a Jew's harp.

His fellow jacks would walk in looking fairly normal and within the span of an hour or so were either fighting or sleeping. The cheap whiskey took it's toll on most of them. The ladies of the night were there also with thoughts of earning a few lumberjack dollars.

One of the painted ladies came up to the group and asked if she could sit with them. Sam moved over and to his surprise, she sat right down in his lap. It might not have been so bad, but Sam had taken his Saturday night bath and he didn't smell too bad. The odor from this hussy made him look for an escape route. He excused himself to go and sit at the bar and when he looked back, there was one of his buddies in a lip lock with her. He was quite amused and just sat and watched. Within a half hour, they both headed up the stairs.

Sam walked back to the table to join his buddies joking about the one upstairs. None of them were drinkers but they sure did enjoy watching the ones that did. There were a few fights and a couple of card games, but the center of the entertainment was watching the ladies claim their victims. Within 20 minutes, their friend was back sitting at the table with a kind of sheepish look on his face, and his woman was on the hunt for another victim.

"How much did that cost you?" asked Sam.

"Well, it was ten spot and darned sure worth it!"

"We'll see." said Sam. "I hope that you didn't pick up anything from her."

Next Wednesday found the intrepid lover of the ladies at the pharmacy trying to purchase something to cure a newly discovered malady. He was desperate for anything to relieve his symptoms and the druggist  grinned at him and collected his money. The embarrassment faded some by the weekend, but he stayed in camp just the same.

The owner of the camp came to Sam early one morning at breakfast asking him if he wanted a new job. Sam hadn't been there very many weeks and was surprised to see the owner walk up to him. Mr. Withers was a big man but didn't look at all like the timber baron he'd heard about.

"Sam, we need you to run a new job for us. We're taking on a big area about 50 miles from here and I need a good foreman. We'll be setting up a complete camp and that means bunkhouses, cook shacks, blacksmith shop and a building for all the stock. What do you think?"

Sam rolled it around in his head for a while and thought that he might like a new job.

"Will I be able to pick my own men?"

"Sure Sam. You can take ten from this camp to get you started and when all the buildings are done I want you to do the rest of the hiring."

"How much are you offering me for a job like this?" asked Sam.

"Well, I had figured on $50.00 a week, but I'll give you more if you earn it. This is going to be a tough job and you'll have to get the respect of your men or you won't be worth plug nickel to me."

"I'll do it Mr. Withers. When do you want me to start?"

"Today will be just about right."

With that, Sam walked outside. He'd only been here a short time and won the respect of the owner and the foreman, both. He was somewhat pleased with himself but he realized the job was going to be a tough one. Picking his first crew was going to be the hardest part. They all had to have experience building with logs and that meant taking the boys from the Bigfork River and a few more.

He walked back into the cook shack and jumped up on a bench.

"I'm looking for a few good men to build a new camp. The work will be hard, six days a week. Pay's about the same as you make now. I need men to build cabins and shacks, a whole camp. Any takers?"

The men looked at each other and then looked over to Tom Anderson to see what he was doing. He sat there looking at Sam, not saying anything. Then he spoke up.

"And who in the hell do you think you are?"

"Well Tom, I'm the one that's going to pay you each Saturday. I'm the one you're going to answer to if you don't give me a day's work and I'm the one that's going to kick your ass if you give me any trouble."

The place went real quiet and Tom slowly got up and walked toward the door. For a minute it looked like he was going to quit and leave camp but he stopped when he reached the door.

"I guess it's time I show you where the bear shit in the buckwheat.

Let's see what you're made of boy."

Tom Anderson went to pull the cook shack door open and the camp foreman walked right in. He sized up the situation in short order and grinned.

"Looks like you two young roosters need to see who's toughest. Well, get on with it and then get back to work."

The cook shack emptied out and the foreman walked inside and poured a cup of hot coffee.

"Got any cinnamon rolls left Cookie?"

He sat and ate his breakfast while all hell broke loose outside. The cook wanted to go and see the excitement, but the foreman kept making small talk with him.

"What you cooking for supper tonight?"

The cook looked all agitated and had a hard time answering the question.

"We're having roast deer meat and taters" he said.

The sounds were growing in intensity outside, but the foreman acted like nothing was happening. Then everything went quiet. He took his last gulp of coffee and walked to the door. The sight that greeted him was one to behold. The crowd was gathered around in a big circle. On the ground lay Tom Anderson, a bit of blood coming from his nose and the makings for two big shiners. Sam grabbed a bucket of water and poured it over Tom's head. He looked a bit worse for wear himself.

He walked over to a stump and stepped up onto it.

"Now, as I was saying, I need 10 good men. Any takers?"

The boys from Minnesota came up to him and said they'd give it a go. Then a few others came and said that they had built camps before. That gave him nine. Then Tom Anderson came up and said that he'd like to give it a try. Sam looked at him and extended his hand.

"Sounds good to me, Tom. We leave tomorrow at dawn."

With that, Sam became the boss. No man questioned his authority. He worked along with his men daylight to dark and the camp started to take shape. Within three months it was complete, except for the cook shack. They needed all the hardware yet, and that included a huge cookstove. The men still were working on the inside of the barn so Sam took a trip to town to order what was still needed. Then he left a note on the bulletin board at the General Store.

"Wanted: One damned good Camp cook, 2 cookies, 50 good jacks, 1 blacksmith, 1 teamster, 1 saw filer. No bums, no drunks and no slackards. See Sam at the Bad Mountain Camp."

Then he headed for the Post Office. He needed to send a postcard to Wil and Ma and one to Missy. He wanted them to know how he was and to let them know how he was doing in his new job. The postmaster took the cards and stamped them.

"Any mail for me back there?" asked Sam.

"Yup. Been holding this now for nearly a month."

He handed Sam a package and it was from Missy. He walked out to the truck and opened it up. It was filled with cookies packed in popcorn and on top was a letter. He opened it slowly. She told of her job at the camp and her friend Peter. She also told about Ma and Wil, and at the very end she said that one of the men had been giving her some trouble, but Peter took care of it. That left him a bit concerned since he felt very protective of his sister.

# CHAPTER 6
## LIFE ON THE RIVER

Back on the Bigfork River, Wil was still in the process of harvest. The garden had done well with the frequent summer rains and hot nights. Ma had canned many quarts of vegetables and fruit so that there would be a good variety of food during the winter. She had grown used to all Missy's help in the kitchen and missed her greatly. They had gotten a lot of wild rice on the river so that gave them a bit of extra money as well.

A knock on the door one evening brought old friend Bill Parsons looking for a hunting partner. He asked Wil if he could get away on Saturday to do some duck hunting on one of the local lakes. Wil looked at him closely, trying to figure if he was sober or not.

A couple years ago Wil had agreed to hunt with him and it turned out to be a rather unforgettable trip. Bill had shown up in the early morning in his truck loaded with decoys and he was just as loaded as the truck. He hadn't even been home yet from his latest trip to the local saloon. He was quite a drinker and Wil had little patience for imbibers. Bill had never married, most likely because he couldn't find anyone that would put up with him.

As Wil went to put his gear in the back of the truck, he heard someone speak and it was his latest drinking companion still loaded to the hilt. Her name was May and the local joke was always "May or May not." This time it looked like "may". She was going to be their hunting companion for the day.

Wil thought to just forget the whole thing, but his word was good and he went along to see how things would go. She was huddled up in the sacks of decoys and had apparently found a comfortable place to get some sleep. Wil threw in his shotgun and his sandwich. This accomplished they headed down the road in the dark looking for Little Jessie Lake.

Wil wasn't paying too close of attention to where they were heading so when they got to the lake, it didn't quite look right to him.

In the dark, they got the boat out of the truck and loaded it up with the decoys. May found a soft spot in the boat and Wil started to row, Bill snoring in the back. It was getting somewhat lighter and he found a spot in the reeds to set up his spread. The decoys were put out and Wil rowed back again into the reeds.

The sun was starting to lighten the fall sky and all of a sudden the ducks started to come towards them in large flocks. Wil brought his 12 gauge to his shoulder and took down the first big mallard. When the gun went off May jumped up and started to swing her fists like she was in a prize fight with an imaginary enemy. The first left caught Bill full on the chin and down he went into the bottom of the boat. She looked down at him and started to giggle. Wil couldn't figure out what was so funny. Enemy defeated, May laid back down and soon was sleeping again.

Wil was having a good shoot and the combatants slept through the whole thing. Around 10 a.m. the excitement had faded some and Wil decided to pick up the decoys and the ducks. He had shot 6 nice mallards and that was a good day as far as he was concerned. Then he headed for the truck or at least where he thought the truck was. As he looked around, he came to the conclusion that he had no idea which lake he was on and Bill was in no shape to tell him. It darned sure wasn't Little Jessie and he couldn't figure what lake it was. He rowed for a long time around the lake and finally saw a mark in the sand where they had pushed the boat into the water. On closer inspection, he had indeed found the truck and he pulled up on shore. He looked down at Bill and he was still asleep or knocked out, he wasn't sure which. He looked at May and she was asleep too, still with a big grin on her face.

Wil gave a shake to his sleeping partner and in time he came around enough to open his eyes.

"Are we dare yet Willy my boy?" asked Bill.

"Why you old fart, I been shooting ducks all morning! How's your chin?"

"What do ya mean Wil?" he asked.

"About four hours ago, May knocked you one in the chops and you been out ever since."

"May who?" he grumbled softly.

"Why you old scutter! You picked her up in the bar last night and brought her along with us hunting this morning."

"Naw! I didn't do that! Did I?" he said a bit perplexed.

It turned out that May had gotten drunk and when it was time to close the place, she crawled into the truck and fell asleep. Bill had been too drunk to even notice her. So as it turned out, May went duck hunting with them and didn't even know it. Wil never forgot that whole thing and whenever Bill asked him to hunt, he had some rather dramatic flashbacks of a time he'd rather forget.

Wil declined the offer to hunt with Bill stating that he had to put up some more hay. He had no desire to hunt with Bill anymore.

At last the hay was all in the barn and it appeared that he had enough to last him until spring and green grass. He was going to winter about the same amount of stock as he had for the last couple years.

Mornings were starting to show small patches of frost in the shaded areas and the local mosquito population had long since vanished. The cold weather also meant that it was time to butcher. He had a nice steer that he had been fattening and now needed to see if Milo at the General Store would buy some of it. There was far too much for the two of them.

He asked Milo to help and between the two men, the beef was

processed and headed for the store for sale. Everyone knew that Wil raised good beef so there was a ready market for his efforts. Ma canned much of the meat and had it ready for winter use.

One afternoon Wil noticed that the wind had changed direction and it was a bit colder. The clouds seemed to be moving in a kind of confused manner. He had been to the barn to check on the stock and when he came back outside, things seemed different. He looked at the sky and couldn't see anything that looked unusual. Out on the river, there were some small waves, but that was normal too. It felt different, like a heavy rock about to fall into the water, like something was about to happen.

In the barn he could hear the milk cows making a bit of noise. Altogether, there was something strange about the day but he couldn't put his finger on it. He walked to the house and checked the barometer. It was way down and that meant a storm was brewing. Ma said that he was imagining things. His years of experience told him that he was right and she wouldn't have to wait long to see for herself.

After a cup of coffee with Ma he put his coat and hat on and headed out toward the river. What greeted him was one of nature's finest shows. Ducks by the hundreds were winging southward flying low on the water. The were in a hurry and none of them landed. They were being chased by the cold breath of Mother Nature herself. The wind was directly out of the north, the opposite of what it had been an hour ago.

Wil watched for nearly an hour and then the snow and freezing rain started, which ran him off to the barn. The wind started again in earnest and the gusts started to blow small limbs off the trees. This was indeed getting serious. From the time that he first noticed the changes in wind until this moment was only a period of an hour and now it was on his mind whether or not the barn could withstand the storm. The chickens were nowhere to be found, and the pigs too had found a spot to get out of the wind.

Wil walked into the house and a worried wife greeted him at the door.

"You sure were right Wil. This is a bad one."

"That wind is getting close to 60 miles an hour and the temperature is still dropping." said Wil. "The last I looked, it was 6 below zero."

He walked to the window and tried to see the outside thermometer. It was frozen thick with ice. He threw some more wood into the fireplace and could feel the draft sucking the air out of the house. This had the makings of being a severe storm.

By night time, the wind was still blowing hard and it made for some fitful sleep for them both. The storm continued for all of the next day dropping a terrible amount of snow and rain. The wind kept up at a furious rate. Wil had decided in midday to walk out and see what it looked like. The barn was still in one piece and the stock was doing well too. Then he turned to walk around the corner of the cabin. The sight was quite unnerving – the river was flowing upstream, backwards. In all his years he had never heard of such a thing.

He turned back into the wind and went inside the cabin. When he told Ma what he had seen, she had to get dressed and go see for herself. There it was in front of her. The Bigfork River, flowing upstream. She looked at Wil and shook her head, quite perplexed. The wind continued unchecked for all that day.

Next morning, Wil went right to the door and opened it to find a warm breeze again out of the south. The storm was over. They never were able to figure out what kind of a storm they had seen, but the townsfolk swore that the temperature went down to forty below that evening. Some had lost livestock and there were a lot of cases of bad frostbite. Milo had gotten word from the Sheriff's office that several duck hunters hadn't made it home. They all died of exposure. It was an amazing storm but the next day all that remained were a few small limbs thrown around the yard.

Life in the logging camp was starting to look a lot like hard work to Missy. With the advent of cold and heavy snow, a great number of lumberjacks came into the camp. She worked from 3 a.m. to get breakfast and quit at 6 p.m. as soon as the food was put out for the jacks. The cookies finished up the day by cleaning the cook shack and then washed all the dishes. For the little pay they received, there sure was a lot of work for them to do.

Missy had a room of her own in the rear of the cook shack. It was plenty large for one person and the only door out was through the store room and then out into the kitchen. She had learned from Wil how to use handguns and always kept a loaded Colt .32 Special on her night stand.

She had hired a woman to come in and bake pies twice a week and then to help with Sunday dinner. The camp had over 150 jacks and they had to be taken good care of or they would head off to different camps with better food.

One morning when she was especially busy, she heard a ruckus in the cook shack and came around the corner in time to see a large man with long black hair reach down and pull a knife from his boot. He was as fast as lightning and the knife flew straight and true, right into another man's heart. He howled briefly in pain but it looked like he was dead before he hit the floor. All of the others in the place headed for the door and that left Missy, the jack and a dead man. He walked over to the dead lumberjack and pulled his knife from the now still heart, wiping the blood off onto his shirt. Then he slowly bent down and replaced the knife inside his boot. The man turned and looked her straight in the eye. He seemed to be looking for something, perhaps a sign that she recognized him. Then Missy started to scream.

She continued to scream until some men overcame their fear and finally decided to come to her aid. As they came toward the killer, he ran for the side door and out into the dark winter morning. Missy had again seen more than she should ever have had to.

The Sheriff from International Falls came to the camp the next day and tried to get a statement from Missy, but she still couldn't talk. The rest of the men had seen the murder anyway and gave them the name of Brad "Scooter" Sherman as the man who committed the murder. Nobody knew what the argument had been about, but it didn't matter now. One of the best jacks in Minnesota had been killed and nothing would undo that.

Missy was shaken to the core from what she had seen, and took some time off to go back home to Wil and Ma's place on the river.

Wil had heard about the murder, but didn't know that Missy had seen it. She was still very scared that the man would come and try to kill her too, and Wil was ready if anything happened.

They had chased Scooter for a long distance through the woods the day of the murder, but he outdistanced them and in time they gave up the chase. The Sheriff put out a wanted poster on the man, but there were no pictures to go with it. His description was given, but the thing that stuck in everyone's mind was the fact that he carried a boot knife.

Wil remembered Sam's description of the man he had seen on the river after the fire and wondered if this could have been the same man. Then he remembered the day Sam got knocked off the log into the river. He thought for a time about the knife he found near the fire, with the initials B.S. Then he thought about who could have hit him over the head in the woods and stole what he had, but there wasn't a face or name to match.

The next day Wil wrote to Sam in Montana and told him what happened at the camp. He needed to know that Missy had been in danger and may still be. He told of the killer's description and the fact that he carried a boot knife.

Next week Missy was back in camp and everyone was glad to see her, not because she was so special, but because they hadn't had a good meal in several days. She cooked up about 40 pounds of roast beef with onions. There were an awful load of boiled potatoes and gallons of gravy. She made 30 loaves of fresh bread and her helper made some baked apples for dessert. All in all the men were pretty glad she was back where she should be. Each and every man there gave her a big grin that evening. No talking was allowed, but they couldn't talk with their mouths that full, anyway.

Toward evening the next day, the Sheriff again pulled into the camp and walked into the cook shack. He had news about Scooter and it wasn't good. It seems that he had robbed a nice old couple about 20 miles north of Missy's camp and in the process, killed them both. The Sheriff said that it was one of the most brutal killings that he had ever seen. Their throats were cut from ear to ear. It appeared that he had stolen all of their money and a lot of food. One horse and saddle was missing as well and that gave him the ability to move around more. The killer wouldn't go hungry. He'd kill for what he wanted and that scared a lot of folks.

"Missy, I know ya can't talk, but I'm darned worried about you here in camp." said the Sheriff. "That man could do nearly anything and I worry about you here. Wil said that you can take care of yourself, but this is a real bad one."

She looked at him for a bit and smiled. Young Peter had been hovering around her since this happened and he would watch out for her. She poured the Sheriff a cup of strong coffee and handed him a sinker to go with it.

Later when the dinner horn sounded, the men came on the run as usual, but this time Peter was at the head of the herd and found himself a spot in the corner where he could see the whole room. He ate slowly, not ready to leave until the last man was gone. Right after the killing, Peter had gone to town and bought a short barreled Colt revolver. He also bought a shoulder holster so nobody knew he was carrying the gun. Most of his time in camp was spent in the supply shack where he kept all of the books for the owners. He had a good view of the cook shack and could see most of the bunkhouses as well. It seemed like a direct contradiction to him between his duties as a Sky Pilot and the fact that he would kill anyone that tried to hurt Missy. He would learn to deal with it in time he was sure.

# CHAPTER 7
## SAM'S CAMP

Mr. Withers was at the camp early one morning and looked up Sam to see if he was ready to start work yet.

"Sam, you did a great job here. This looks a lot like the camps I've seen in Minnesota."

"Well, I guess that's the only way I know to build them. I learned from one of the best there is in log building, Wil Morgan. He lives up on the Bigfork River in Minnesota."

Mr. Withers got a surprised look on his face.

"Why, I knew Wil 30 years ago. He taught me how to hunt and fish when we was kids. I used to spend summers up there on the Bigfork when my dad would get tired of me hanging around the saloons. He'd write to Wil and off I'd go for the summer."

He asked how Wil was and if he ever got married. The answers seemed to please Mr. Withers greatly. He thought it strange how Wil built his cabin right in the same area they used to camp. They would stay sometimes for weeks at a time and catch great numbers of big walleyes and northerns. What a time it was to be a kid! No worries, no problems.

"How are you doing on hiring men?"

"Well, we got the jobs posted on the bulletin boards and in the area General Stores. It might take some time before we can get a good crew, but I expect that we will be running in short order. I've heard that the word got out about us using one-man saws and that we pay pretty darned good money."

"Well, we don't pay any more per cord than any other company, but we work smarter and produce more per day, thanks to you Sam."

"Thank you Mr. Withers. We do have one problem though and that is finding a camp cook. My sister Missy cooks at one and the men love her food. I don't think I could get her to come here, though. Do you have any ideas?"

"Well Sam, I tell you what. If we don't get a good cook, we'll have to cut this timber ourselves. The lumberjacks I've known would rather work for half wages than starve at the hands of a lousy camp cook. We won't get a soul to come up this mountain without a cook."

Sam thought for a bit and then asked how much Mr. Withers was willing to spend.

"Well my boy, Ill leave that up to you. Don't go over $200 a month if you don't have to."

Sam nearly fell over. That was an unheard of amount of money. A chef from New York's finest restaurants would only cost half that amount. So here he sat on top of a Montana mountain looking for a chef that will come and cook for them. Many thoughts ran through his head, but he still had no idea where to start. His small crew was really tired of eating beans and potatoes and he thought that they might mutiny pretty soon.

The next day a few men showed up looking for work so the cutting started even if it was a small operation. They knew there was no cook yet, but they all needed a job.

Sam got into the camp truck and headed down the mountain toward town and the post office. There was no man that knew the goings on in a community better than the Postmaster. He walked in and the man recognized him immediately from the timber camp.

"You're Sam Anderson from the Bad Mountain Camp aren't you?" said the Postmaster.

"Yup that's me alright and I've got a big problem. I sure could use some advice. Mr. Withers told me to hire a camp cook and I don't know where to begin. I need someone who makes the finest camp food in the area, someone who will feed our men like they were  kings. He has to be about the best cook in the state."

"Well, I guess I can't help you." said the bespectacled Postmaster. "I had it all figured out for you until you said that it had to be a man. Sorry Sam."

"What do you mean? Do you know of a woman who could do it?"

"Well, I don't like to brag, but my daughter Mary Jane can beat anyone at cooking. Say, why don't you come to my house for dinner Saturday night and see for yourself? My wife and I would like to show her off to a stranger, anyways. How much will the job pay? She won't work for free ya know?"

"The pay is according to how good a cook she is and that's up to me," said Sam. "Where do you live and what time should I be there?"

"Well, you go south of here about a half mile and turn into a grove of pines on the left. Look for the name Wilson on the mailbox. Come on in whenever you can after 5:00."

The day of the big dinner moved along slowly. Sam went to a few small towns asking about hiring jacks and camp workers, but it seemed that everyone already had good jobs. He had signed only one man in the entire day and when he found out that they didn't have a cook yet, he told Sam to look him up when he got a good cook. He was starting to feel that he might not be able to fill the camp.

It was getting on close to 4:30 and he headed to the Wilson place to see what the cook could do. As he drove into the yard, there was a beautiful young lady hanging clothes on the line and she gave him a big smile. As she walked toward him, Sam got a lump in his throat the size of Texas, and couldn't think of a thing to say.

"I'm Mary Jane," she said, extending her hand.

"I, I, I'm Sam Anderson," he said softly.

"Come in and sit for a bit. Dad will be here shortly. He had to run into town and get some milk for dinner."

"Thank you Ma'am." he stuttered.

Sam had never in his entire life seen the likes of this woman. She was the prettiest, sweetest, nicest and kindest woman he had ever met! She was dressed all in blue with blonde hair and blue eyes to match her dress. He accepted a cup of coffee from her and had to find a place to set it down or his shaking hand would have spilled it all over the floor. He was completely infatuated with this woman.

Soon Mrs. Wilson came into the room and introduced herself to Sam. She too was beautiful and dressed in a long blue dress. He thought that at one time she had been as pretty as her daughter. Then he heard the car come into the yard. He was starting to breathe a bit easier now that Mr. Wilson had arrived. The two men were deep in conversation about the logging business when Mary Jane called them for dinner.

"It's time for you to see for yourself what kind of a cook my daughter is. Come on Sam."

Mr. Wilson walked behind his wife and slid her chair in for her and then motioned for Sam to sit at the opposite end of the table. He had thought to help Mary Jane with her chair, but she was still quite busy in the kitchen. He sat quietly waiting.

"Have you been in the area long, Sam?" asked Mary Jane from the kitchen.

"No Ma'am. It's only been a few months now."

"If you call me Ma'am one more time, I'm going to fill your shirt pocket with gravy," she said laughing.

They all laughed a bit and in walked this most beautiful woman in the world holding a glazed ham all decorated with fresh pineapple and cherries. Then in came a bowl piled high with snow-white mashed potatoes. Then it was glazed carrots followed by little dinner rolls. Again they laughed at Sam because his eyes were wide open and so was his mouth.

"I have never seen anything that even came close to this," said Sam.

Mr. Wilson stood and offered one hand to Sam and the other to his wife. Sam took the hint and held Mary Jane's hand so they were all joined in a circle. The warmth of her soft hand made it difficult to concentrate.

"Would you like to say grace for us Sam?" said Mrs. Wilson.

He was flustered indeed, but he was no stranger to prayer.

"Lord we come to you today asking your blessing on this lovely meal and the family who invited a stranger in from the mountain. We too pray for the family I left behind in Minnesota, Wil, Ma and my sister Missy. Amen"

And with that, Sam began an adventure in fine dining that lasted nearly an hour. He was the guest in a home where fantastic food and good manners were common.

At the end of the meal, they all went into the sitting room and talked of what it was like where Sam was from and to see what he thought of the meal.

"Mary Jane what would you charge to be the head cook for a group of nearly 150 men? There is breakfast, lunch and dinner seven days a week, but you can hire all the help you want. You would have to cook meals that would get the men to talking about you. The word would get out and then our camp would be full of good lumberjacks."

"Do you think that I could have Sundays off? I never work on Sunday."

"You could do whatever you want because you would be in charge of the whole cook shack."

She mused a while and asked Sam if $20.00 a week would be too much.

Sam nearly choked.

"Mary Jane, if you cook like this all the time, I am willing to offer you $200.00 a month.

Then it was her turn to choke. Her face flushed and she just sat there.

"Do you really mean $200.00 a month? I never heard of such a thing!" said Mr. Wilson.

With that the deal was made and the men came from far and wide as they heard about the new cook. She had a team of five cookies and an assistant cook she could use whenever she wanted.

Mr. Withers drove into the camp early one morning looking for the cook he was paying such a large amount of money to each month. None of the men knew who he was, except for a couple so he just walked in like he was one of the men. Near to the door was a menu written in fine handwriting.

Menu de jour:

New Orleans French Quarter Toast with Minnesota Maple Syrup.

West Virginia honey cured ham steaks.

Fried Idaho potatoes.

Stewed Prunes with orange.

Milk.

Buttermilk.

Coffee.

This didn't look too bad to Mr. Withers since he hadn't eaten since the day before. As he went through the food serving line, he was quite impressed by the way the food looked and the cleanliness of the place. As he started to eat, he was most surely surprised by how good it tasted. After he finished, he went back for another helping and was told he'd get something for lunch if he worked hard, but no second helpings. He was somewhat perplexed by being told no by his own employees. Inside he laughed a bit.

He stumbled out the door and ran right into Sam, just the man he was looking for.

"Well, so far it looks like you did another fine job for me, Sam. The camp is full of good men, no fighting and no gambling. All hard working men. I was in the barber shop in Billings and heard about this camp. Some men said that they would work for free if they could just get their meals here."

"Thanks Mr. Withers. She is most certainly the finest cook that anyone has ever known and our production is going way up each week. Besides that, she sure is pretty."

They both laughed.

"Any idea what's for supper Sam?"

Life on the mountain was hard and everyone was expected to

pull his share of the load. Some jobs paid more than others so that set up a kind of a hierarchy. The sawyers got more than the teamsters, and the blacksmith got more than the saw filers. Each job was important, but to pay them all the same was unheard of. Mr. Withers had a problem on his hands and decided to talk to the men face to face the next evening.

There had been talk of the men joining a union so that they would make more money and have some job security.

On the other side of the coin was Mr. Withers, the owner of the camp. He thought that he paid the men well and fed them well, too. He had a hard time understanding the position of the men. He felt that they were ungrateful.

That evening, after the dishes were cleaned and put away the cook's helper blew the horn and the men came from everywhere. Mr. Withers stood up on a box in front of the group and made his speech.

"From what I understand, you men have a complaint about what I am paying for wages. The very first thing is that what I pay the man next to you is his business and not yours. You make a good wage, each and every one of you. I hire good men, expect a hard day's work and you have fulfilled that duty. There is also some talk about you men joining a union. I won't have it and that is the end of that story. The next man that talks union in this camp will be run off my mountain. Now, do you have anyone that is a spokesman for your group?"

A man in the front of the room raised his hand and said that the rest of the men asked him to speak for them. His name was Myron Berg, a really big man with a deep voice.

"Mr. Withers, the first thing I want to say is that all of us appreciate what you pay us and how you treat us so fairly. But the point we want to make is security. If we go out on the mountain tomorrow and get a tree dropped on our head, our families starve and that is a fact we can't walk away from. When we get old and can't run a saw any longer, we starve. If there is no timber to cut, we starve. There is a hundred ways to get killed up here and then it's tough times for our families. We have no complaint about our wages, but we need to take care of our families."

He sat down and Mr. Withers stood again. He looked out over the crowd of men. There wasn't a bad man in the bunch, but what they had to say was true. If they got hurt, they didn't get paid.

"How much money would each man need to get by on if he was hurt?" asked Mr. Withers. "That is at the center of the problem. What you say is quite true, but don't ever think that a union will get it for you. I'd shut down the whole damned camp before I'd let a union man on this mountain. I am a reasonable man and know quite a bit about insurance and investing. Are there any men here that would like to form a group to help solve this problem?"

The men all looked from one to another. There were no businessmen in the group, only hard working men faced with a hard problem. Pretty soon a man in back stood and called out his own name. Then another and another. Soon they had six good men.

"Let me have a week to get some figures together and we'll meet here again in exactly one week. We'll set the group down in front of the room with me and discuss the problem in front of the whole group. No secret meetings." said Mr. Withers.

Next week as scheduled, the time for the meeting arrived. Mr. Withers took the floor.

"This business of security has many faces and with that comes many problems. The first thought was that we forget the whole thing because it would cost too much. On looking closer at the problem, I have come up with an idea that you might like. Do you want to hear about it?"

The spokesman took the floor and said that they had talked for many hours and couldn't come up with anything except the amount they would need each month to get by.

"And how much do you think that would be?" asked Mr. Withers.

"It looks like about $15.00 a month would get us through the bad times. That would be enough to buy food with and a little extra." said the spokesman.

"I had figured about $20.00 a month and the cost is reasonable if we both share the burden." said Mr. Withers. "The cost for each man would be about 50 cents a week and I put in the same amount for each man. Now, this can't be a benefit for just anyone, it's for the men who stick with me. No benefits for the first two years for any man but in the third year, we will issue him an insurance policy that will pay him $20.00 a month if he is out of work due to injury or lay off. If I remember right, it will last for 6 months and that is enough for most men to get back to work. It will give you the protection you wanted."

The men all looked from one to another and felt that it was more than fair. There were a lot of smiles in the crowd. Then Mr. Withers took the floor again.

"Now we have one more point to clear up. What I pay a man for his work is my business and the business of the man earning the wage. There will be no more discussion between you of how much you are making. It causes a lot of bad feelings in the camp and I won't tolerate it. Enough said on that subject. Now, I have heard from good sources that you men don't like the food in this camp. Well, I like it quite well and have gained five pounds from my weekly visits." He patted his newly protruding stomach.

The whole room erupted in laughter. The entire camp loved Mary Jane and with one voice said that they loved the food too.

With that, the meeting adjourned and the cook shack emptied except for Sam and Mary Jane Wilson.

"Care for a cup of coffee Sam?" asked Mary Jane.

"No thanks. That would keep me awake for hours. Got any buttermilk?" asked Sam grinning.

She poured him a large glass full and set it down in front of him.

"Thanks Mary Jane."

She sat down across from him and watched him for a time.

"Would you like to go to the dance with me next Saturday? There's a band playing down in Ramey Junction."

"I'd love to Sam. I really do love to waltz and if there is a polka I'll dance that too."

Sam was surprised at his own boldness asking such a pretty woman for a date, but this time he meant business. This was the prettiest woman he had ever met and he had plans for her.

"Where can I pick you up?"

"I'll be at my parents' house. You'll have to come in and talk to my dad for a bit. What time are you going to pick me up?"

"I'll be there at 8:00 and the dance starts at 9:00 so that will give us plenty of time." said Sam.

Inside, his heart was racing, but hers was too. Each of them had been looking at the other to make a move and now the deed was done.

Saturday found Sam at work on the mountain and at 4:00 he headed back to camp to get cleaned up. He found an old wash tub and boiled up some water for a tub bath, a real rarity in this camp. He scrubbed up thoroughly and trimmed his mustache neatly. A small dab of Brilliantine made his hair shine. He didn't look too bad for a lumberjack.

He drove the company pickup truck to town and into the Wilson's yard at the appointed time. Mrs. Wilson came to the door and invited him inside.

"Come in and sit for a bit. Mary Jane will be out in a short while," said Mrs. Wilson.

"Thank you," said Sam. "Where is Mr. Wilson?"

He didn't have long to wait until he came into the room.

"Hello Sam," he said removing his glasses. "How have you been?"

"I'm doing great and staying real busy."

With that Mary Jane walked into the room. She was magnificent and her blonde hair was tied back and very pretty too. Sam was having a bit of a time trying to think of something to say.

"Now you remember, I want her back home before 11:00 tonight."

"Yes sir. I'll have her home on time," said Sam. And with that they walked out to the truck.

Sam opened the door for her, using his very best manners. As soon as his door closed, Mary Jane started to laugh. It appeared as if her dad was going to eat him alive but he was very protective of his only daughter. They both felt somewhat more relaxed now that they were out on the road and headed for the dance.

As time went on, their dates became more frequent and the Wilson family thought of Sam as a possible suitor for their daughter. He ate many Sunday dinners at their house and it seemed that Mr. Wilson was even starting to like Sam a bit more.

One Sunday, Sam and Mr. Wilson were in the sitting room talking. Sam got a real serious look on his face.

"Mr. Wilson, I'd like to marry your daughter."

There. The deed had been done. He had pondered long and hard on how he was going to say it, but it all came out at once. He said that he had plans to start his own timber camp one day and he'd try his very best to be a good husband to her.

Mr. Wilson kind of figured that this would happen one day and was glad that it was Sam. He was a hard worker and that meant a lot to him.

So in the spring of the year, Sam and Mary Jane stood on a spot overlooking the great Wind River. It was a beautiful day and a warm breeze blew through bride's hair making the whole sky look golden. Sam stood looking into the eyes of the prettiest woman in the world telling her that he would always love her, that he would always be faithful and that he would always be there for her. She did the same and with a tender kiss they became man and wife, the lumberjack and the camp cook.

The Sheriff's office in International Falls Minnesota was normally a pretty quiet place, but in the last few weeks it took on a somewhat different look. The Royal Canadian Mounted Police or R.C.M.P. was called in since the murder at the lumber camp involved a sometimes Canadian citizen. The name Brad Sherman was passed from man to man in the office and each officer got to know who he was and what he was capable of.

The murder of that old couple really had a lot of folks pretty scared. A man that could commit that kind of a crime might do about anything. The Sheriff had spent a lot of time on this case. The thoughts of him still being around bothered a lot of people. Even the school kids weren't allowed to go to school alone.

There were wanted posters posted at all of the lumber camps and all the stores and gas stations in the area.

A large man came into the Brush Creek Camp one evening looking for work. He had a neatly trimmed beard and very short hair. He claimed to have worked at a lot of camps, but none of the men knew him. His name was Bill Boyers. The foreman decided to give him a try because he was so darned hard up for men. The Brush Creek camp was only a few miles from the one Missy was at, and like most camps was right on the Bigfork River.

One evening a few men started to get up a card game and the stakes were getting up where only a few could afford to play. The new man, Bill Boyers was losing some money and making it clear that he didn't like it much. One pot was getting pretty high and when he lost, he overturned the table and everything went flying. He and another jack went chest to chest and Bill Boyers grinned and backed down. He acted like it was no big thing and he walked outside to roll a cigarette. It was pretty cold out and he stayed for just a short time and went back in. He wanted his money back but the men wouldn't let him in the game. This angered him greatly and he had a hard time not reacting. He walked to his bunk and crawled in for the night.

He lay there thinking about what he could do to get his money back without drawing attention to himself.

The next morning in the cook shack he had it figured out. A slight grin crossed his face, but only for a moment. He continued to eat.

His target was Swede, a big, good natured man. He held in his pocket about $7.00 of Boyer's money and he was determined that he would get it back.

The morning found the crew spread out in a big stand of Red Pines. There were some unusually large trees and the men were all working hard. Boyer's idea was to drop one on Swede when he wasn't looking. Then he thought that if anyone saw him do it, the jig would be up for him for sure. Then he had a better idea. He would sneak up behind him and hit him with a large branch so that it looked like one fell out of the tree he was sawing. The plan was set and he proceeded toward Swede, as quietly as he could. He picked up a large branch about four feet long and about six inches thick. He raised it high and at that moment one of the crew saw what was happening and yelled at Swede to duck. He did and turned at the same time to see his attacker. Boyers was caught red-handed attempting to murder a fellow lumberjack. The fight was on and Swede was a scrapper from the old country. Each time that Boyers got in close enough to use the chunk of wood he held, Swede would pile right in close and hammer him hard with his giant fists. He knocked Boyers down to the ground but he came up with his knife drawn and it looked like Swede was about to get cut bad. At this stage in the fight, all Boyers really wanted was to put as much distance between him and Swede as possible so at his first chance, he threw a handful of snow into Swede's face and started to run for the bunkhouse.

Swede thought to follow him, but he figured that getting away without needing to get sewed up was enough of a victory for today. He'd talk to the foreman when it was lunch time.

When the swingdingle made its appearance, the men all headed to get something to eat and a cup of coffee. The foreman was sitting on a stump eating when Swede went up to him.

"You look a little worse for wear today." said the foreman.

"Ya I guess so," said Swede. "I think that new guy tried to kill me this morning. I was cutting in the big pines and he tried to club me over the head with a log. If Ole hadn't seen him and warned me, I'd be a dead man right now."

"What the hell are you talking about?"

"Ya. Das right," said Ole. "He had the log up over Swede's head when I saw him and I yelled."

"I got a feeling that there is more to this story so let's hear it," said the foreman.

"Well, we was playing a little cards last night and that Boyer got mad when he lost some money," said Swede.

"I told you no gambling in camp," said the foreman. "I'm going to look in on that Boyers and see what he has to say. Anybody seen him?"

A couple of men had seen him heading for the camp so the foreman headed there too. He was determined to see what Boyers had to say. When he got there, he found all of Boyers' stuff was gone and he was, too.

Then as he came out of the bunkhouse, he saw the Sheriff pull in and shut off the motor.

"Did you get that wanted poster I sent you?" he asked. "That Brad Sherman is a bad one."

"No. I didn't get to town for the mail this week. We been pretty busy here."

With that the Sheriff pulled out another poster and the foreman's blood chilled when he read the description. They had Brad "Scooter" Sherman in their camp for nearly a week and didn't even know it. He was suspected in a double murder of an old couple not far from their camp. That man had been here in their midst and through their own good fortune, nobody had been killed.

Word again was spread from camp to camp about Scooter and they all kept an eye out for him. Then nearly a week after he left the logging camp, someone tried to get across the border in International Falls without any identification. The guards had held him for a few hours because he matched the description on the wanted posters, but let him go when he convinced them that he was a traveling preacher. They, however, didn't let him into Canada because he had no identification. It seemed that he could change his identity at will and do so convincingly.

Wil and Ma had gotten word about Brad Sherman and were a bit perplexed by the fact that he would stay here in the area. It seemed that everyone in the valley knew him or knew about him, so there was nowhere he could run unless he crossed the border into Canada.

One day as Wil was walking toward the barn, he looked up into the trees and was somewhat fascinated by what he saw. The ground was fully covered with deep snow and the contrast of one old oak tree made him stop for a second look. The tree had nothing green on it, there was no hope of spring. It was a stark reminder of how cold and desolate this country was in winter. The tree looked like it was stuck in one position even though it wanted to be blown around by warm breezes. Birds nesting in its branches were a long way off yet.

He entered the barn and it was the same there. All the animals were suspended in time, waiting for spring and green grass. Some of the sheep seemed to be getting closer to lambing and that at least gave Wil some hope of warmer weather. This time of year, anything could happen with the weather.

Ma too was impatient for warmer weather. Her thoughts turned to things like garden seed and spring flowers. This time of year people had about all of the winter they could stand.

Early one morning, Wil asked Ma if she would like to go along to the store and pick up some supplies. He had some feed to pick up and they both needed to catch up on the local news. It had been some time since they checked the mail too.

"Hey Jack! Hey Topsy! Giddup!"

The team gave a hard surge forward and down the road they went at a fast trot, the wind blowing through Ma's blonde hair. The warm wind of spring was in the air and it felt good to both of them. As they neared the main road, Wil slowed the team and made a wide turn to the left, away from the store. The team loved to pull and they hadn't been out of the barn much because of the bad winter storms.

They had gone a couple miles and Wil turned out into a large field and that made the team work hard in the deep snow. Then they were back out onto the road headed for town. The horses had thrown a lot of snow up onto them and they were covered with white. As they neared the General Store, they slowed down to a slow walk. Then they stopped and tied up at the hitch.

As they entered the store, they heard Milo yell to Ann.

"Look here Ann. We got a new family in the valley."

"Hello Milo," said Wil. "I guess it's been quite a while since we were to town."

He went up and shook Milo's hand and Ann came out and gave Ma a hug. These were good friends and each was glad to see their neighbors.

"We got some mail here for you folks, too," said Ann. "It's from some people in Montana named Mr. and Mrs. Sam Anderson."

Ma got a big grin on her face and went over to claim the letter. She looked it over front and back and placed it securely inside of her purse.

Wil picked up a couple cans of peaches and a new battery for the old Zenith radio. Ma got a few sewing notions and a pound of her favorite, horehound candy. Then Wil headed to the feed store. He needed some scratch for the chickens and a couple bags of cracked corn.

Then it was off down the road to the only restaurant for many miles. Ma was a far better cook than anyone in the valley but it sure was nice to have someone wait on them. They each ordered apple pie and coffee. There were a few old friends there and they stayed a while just for the conversation. It seemed to be a good place to catch up on the local happenings. It seemed that people were feeling the need to peek outside and see if spring had arrived yet.

After the trip home, and the horses taken care of, they went inside to read the letter. Ma handed it to Wil since reading was always a problem for her and she had little schooling. He opened the envelope carefully and removed two sheets of paper.

Sam and Mary Jane were both doing well and like them were impatient about seeing spring. Then they told about how their camp was doing well and how they were able to save quite a bit of money. Then at the very end of the letter they said that they were going to become parents and that this would be no kind of a life for a baby. They also said that Mary Jane would have to stop all the heavy lifting she had been doing as camp cook. They closed sending their love and asked that they tell Missy about the good news.

Ma sat there for a while wondering about the letter they had just read. There was no mention of where they would go since they couldn't work in the lumber camps. Ma thought that Sam might get a job in a nearby town but Wil figured that Sam had sawdust in his veins and would stay in the timber business one way or another. The discussion went on for a couple more hours until Wil had to go do the chores and Ma had to make some supper. All in all it had been quite a day.

Wil looked up and saw Ma sitting there dabbing at the tears welling in her eyes. This was surely good news for them both.

The next day Wil and Ma decided to hitch up the team and head to the camp that Missy was working at. She had to be told the good news. The trip was over 8 miles each way and they packed sandwiches for the trip. Their youngster was now nearly 2 and still being breast fed so his lunch was taken care of already. At 6 a.m. they were headed down the road throwing up a spray of mud and gravel. Spring was getting much closer and the ground was starting to get a bit softer in the areas that the sun shined on.

As they traveled along the river trail towards the camp they watched closely for signs that the rafts of timber had started their trip. The big timber camps had large piles of logs lined along the river bank and when the river started to run, they would let loose the big rafts of timber to be floated to the mills further down river. There was always the problem of log jams but the men did their best to keep the great mass of timber moving. These men were called "river pigs". Their job was the most dangerous of all in the timber industry. They used long pike poles to stop potential log jams. Once in a while when the logs moved too fast, a man would get sucked under the mass of timber and never be seen again.

As they got closer to the camp they saw that the timber was already on the move. Great plumes of river water sailed skyward at the rapids. Wil and Ma stopped and watched for a while as the river pigs tried in vain to open a bad log jam. After quite a bit of work, they had decided to use dynamite.

One of the men walked way out on the jam carrying a whole case of dynamite. The jam was growing as the timber behind kept the pile growing. He set the wooden case down and fished in his pocket for a match to get the fuse going. This accomplished he started to run for a safer place to watch from. He had covered nearly a hundred yards when the blast threw logs high in the air and the man went down on his face in the water. He immediately got up and finished his run to the shore. The logs all came crashing down around him and Wil and Ma watched the whole show. This was indeed dangerous work but men needed jobs and this was one that paid a living wage.

As the big raft of logs once again started moving they made a terrible grinding noise you could hear for a long distance. This was a job that Wil had done in his earlier days but it was usually left for men without families.

A wannigan would follow the log raft down stream and provide meals for the jacks. The food wasn't anything as good as what they got at camp but a hot meal was just the same, much appreciated.

"Remember the old days when I used to do that Ma?" Wil asked.

"Sure, but there was a lot of times I wondered if you'd ever come back."

"It was dangerous work for sure but jobs were hard to find back then."

As they got close to the camp, they noticed more and more men walking along the roads with their bags. This was the end of the season for most of the men. The camp needed frozen roads to move the logs and with breakup it was the end until next freeze. The big camps emptied out and everyone headed back home. Wil was sure that Missy would be done soon.

They pulled the wagon into the camp and walked into the cook shack. It was usually a nice warm place, but today it was dark and cold. The fire in the big cook stove had gone out and all of the kerosene lamps were dark as well. This was the last place to quit at a camp.

Wil gave out a loud yell for Missy and she came out from her room in the back, all full of smiles. She waved for them to come in. As they entered the room, they saw that she had been busy packing her things. There wasn't much, but still there were a few bags to be loaded.

Ma sat down at her little table with the baby and started to tell about Sam and Mary Jane's new baby. Missy was excited and a bit frustrated. She had so much to say and nothing would come out. Tears gathered in her eyes and she wiped them away with her sleeve.

Missy went to Ma and took the baby from her. She made faces and the youngster responded as if he remembered her.

"Are ya comin' home with us Missy?" asked Ma. "It sure would be nice to have ya home with us for the summer."

Missy looked at them and nodded yes. She first went to Ma and gave her a big hug and then over to Wil. He was somewhat embarrassed but managed to keep his composure.

They got everything loaded into the wagon and Missy got in the back and held the baby, all wrapped up in flannel blankets. The temperature was still only in the low 40's and so with the wind in their faces, they headed back to their home on the river.

Missy and the baby shared the room and it seemed to suit her well. The boy didn't wake up at night any more so the whole house got a good night's sleep.

# CHAPTER 8
## MOUNTAIN LOGGING

Sam was hard at work at the Bad Mountain camp. His days were spent more on management than on doing the jobs he loved like cutting timber. Mr. Withers had given him a raise to $75.00 a week and with it came a whole pile of new responsibilities. He was getting close to shutting down for the summer and had already laid off many of the men. They had all said that they would come back again as soon as the weather cooled down. Summer was no friend to a lumberjack.

One day while Sam was going over the books, Mr. Withers walked in and sat down at Sam's desk.

"My boy, we gotta have a talk."

That was usually the start of a pretty serious conversation like when he had to fire someone or they weren't making the money he figured they should. Sam braced himself for the worst.

Mr. Withers reached into his file cabinet and pulled out a bottle of his favorite, peppermint schnapps. He poured them each a small amount and raised his glass in a toast to Sam.

"My boy, you have done one hell of a fine job for me. Here's to you."

He raised his glass to Sam and they drank it down. Sam was a bit perplexed at the bosses kind words.

"Thank you Mr. Withers. I appreciate that."

"Well, now that I have embarrassed you sufficiently, I have a proposition for you. I want you to go and build a new camp for me."

"Mr. Withers, I don't think that I can do it. Mary Jane is pregnant and the baby will arrive near February first. She won't be able to do any lifting for quite some time."

Sam held his head low and didn't know quite what to say.

"I think we're going to head back to Minnesota. I might try to start a camp of my own some day," said Sam.

Mr. Withers poured them another shot of schnapps. This time they just sipped on it, making small talk about babies and camp cooks.

"Funny how things seem to work out sometimes," said Mr. Withers.

He kept grinning at Sam and he wasn't quite sure if the schnapps had gotten to Mr. Withers or if there was more to be said.

"I got a letter today from an old friend in Minnesota that I have been dealing with. He found a parcel of land running as near as I can figure, 14,000 acres of prime red pine. There are four streams that run through it and eventually they come to the Bigfork River. The price is higher than I wanted to pay, but a big company from Minneapolis is wanting it, too. Today I got word that my bid has been accepted."

Mr. Withers was still grinning from ear to ear, and Sam still didn't get what was so funny.

"I want you to stick with me when we open the Minnesota camp Sam and even more importantly, I want your fine wife to be in charge of the cooks. She can hire and fire and do all of the buying. She won't have to cook any more. Then I want to hire Wil Morgan, my old friend to help get the crews hired. Nobody knows more people than him."

Sam was standing there with his empty glass in his hand, not saying anything. Then Mr. Withers decided to wait him out and see what would happen. They stared at each other for quite a while and then it seemed that Sam found his voice once more.

"I'll have to talk to my wife about this, but I do have to say that you've taken me somewhat by surprise. We want to go to back to Minnesota and if that new area is anywhere near where I think it is, we'll have our work cut out for us. I can do the job for sure, but we'll have to get right at building the first camp or we won't be able to cut timber next winter. I'll also need the men I brought from Minnesota when I came here. Sure would like to have Tom Anderson, too, if he'd want to move with us."

He and Tom Anderson had become good friends and Sam knew he was a hard worker.

Once again, Mr. Withers had his man. He offered a job to Sam and it gave him a chance to move him and his wife to the new location and keep the job he loved. He had a reputation of being a loyal worker who got the job done.

Sam told Mary Jane about the job offer at dinner that night. There was no talk about pay but they both knew that Mr. Withers was more than fair with the pay. She would be responsible for around five camps. That was indeed a big job, but she knew she could do it. She, above everything else, wanted to be near her husband and the new child.

They had everything packed in three days and using the new company truck, headed back to Minnesota. Mary Jane's family would sure miss her, but they planned to visit as often as they could.

One afternoon Wil had gone to the General Store to get some nails, and Milo had a post card for him. It was from Montana, but he didn't recognize the name. The writing was quite sloppy and he asked Milo to help him make out the writing. The card read:

Dear Wil,

 Coming shortly to your neck of the woods. Have a job offer for you. Are the walleyes still biting?

Best Regards,
Wilbur

That made no sense to Wil and he didn't know anyone there other than Sam. Ma looked at the card and handed it back to Wil.

"We don't know anyone else there, do we?" said Ma.

"No. I can't figure it out and that handwriting is a mess. The name looks like Walker or Walter"

That night after the dishes were done and Ma had the baby taken care of, Wil stood and walked to the fireplace. He put a couple logs on the fire and threw a couple pieces of firewood into the Monarch cook stove.

"I'm tuckered out. Good night Missy. Good night Ma."

And with that, he walked into the bedroom, put on his nightshirt and covered up for the night. The house was settling down and everyone was getting ready for bed. Within a few minutes, Ma came in and she too, covered up for the night.

Missy was still sitting by the fireplace reading her Bible as she always did before bed time. She heard Ma start to snore softly and smiled.

Then out of nowhere, Wil sat up in bed and shouted "Wilbur Withers, it's Wilbur Withers"

Missy nearly fell out of the rocker and the baby started to cry.

"Wil Morgan if you ever do that again you might end up raising our young 'un all by yourself. Now what in the world is a Wilbur Withers?"

Wil told her about his friend from so long ago. His father was a businessman from out east and each time Wilbur got a bit out of control, he'd send him to spend the summer with Wil on the Bigfork River. They had been close friends several years ago.

Once again the house settled down and the sounds of soft breathing came to the little cabin on the Bigfork River. A slight grin then came to rest on the face of the now slumbering Wil Morgan.

Daylight found Wil trying to warm up the house. He again threw some wood into the cookstove and had a pot of coffee going in no time. Wil was convinced that his heart didn't even start beating until he had his second cup. On this day he was a bit more cheerful than usual. Ma came into the kitchen and sat down with Wil.

"Now tell me about this Wilbur Withers." said Ma.

"Well, as far back as I can remember, Wilbur was a good friend.

Not quite sure how I came to know him, but he was there from the time I was just a pup. His Pa would send him to us for the summer and we ran the countryside like wild animals. Sometimes we'd just stop wherever we were for the night, build a fire and cover up with balsam branches to keep warm. We ate nearly anything that could be called food but it was mostly fish and berries.

"Sometimes we just moved from one Indian camp to the next just seeing kids that were our age, then off we'd go to the next adventure. If I remember right, one time we stayed gone for two weeks and when we got back home, we looked pretty bad. Our hair was long and we hadn't fallen in the river for quite a while. My father said that we weren't going to get fed 'til we cleaned up some. Didn't matter to us anyway cuz we never went hungry.

"One time Wilbur had brought a new 30-30 rifle with him and that meant that we could get some real meat. Well, we hadn't been too lucky at hunting and the berry crop had failed something terrible. We tried hard to catch some fish and even that didn't work out for us. We were getting close to heading home for some food.

"So one morning while I was sitting by the fire, Wilbur grabbed his gun and said that he'd be back before noon. I sat there for quite a while by the river trying to catch a fish and nothing would cooperate. Some time a couple of hours after he left, I heard a single gunshot. That didn't bother me much cuz Wilbur was a pretty good shot. The direction it came from was up river a ways. Well, I sat there for another hour and still no sign of Wilbur.

"When it got to be around noon, I decided to go and look for him. I put the canoe in the water and started to paddle up stream. I had gone about a mile and I heard the sound of Wilbur yelling. I pulled the canoe in to shore and started to follow his voice. He just kept yelling "Wil! ".

"Well, I finally started to get a bit closer and I entered a small clearing. There was Wilbur, about 30 feet up in a popple tree, yelling at the top of his lungs for me. Then I saw the nature of his problem. The bear was bleeding from a shot high on her shoulder. Then over about 50 feet up in a tree was a pair of this years cubs. I just kept quiet for a while, watching. Wilbur's gun was lying on the ground by the tree and the bear kept climbing up and down the tree, trying to get at his legs.

"In a few minutes, the bear came back down the tree to go check on her cubs. As she went up a different tree, I ran in and got Wilbur's gun. The big she- bear looked at me and decided that now the odds had changed and it wasn't in her favor. She gave a soft "woof" and the cubs came down and followed her slowly into the brush.

Then it was Wilbur's turn to come down. The sow had gotten up close enough to him that she tore off his shoe and chewed it up quite a bit. He recovered the remains of it and we headed back to the river. Wilbur swore that he'd never shoot at another bear no matter how hungry he got. We had a lot of adventures, but that was one that could have turned out much differently."

By the time he had finished his story, Missy was there and the baby was happily chewing on a piece of toast. Wil heard someone drive into the yard and opened the door to see a truck pull in with the name "Bad Mountain Timber Co." printed on the door. He looked at the driver and it took a second before he recognized him. It was Sam.

"Well Sam!" said Wil. "What a surprise!"

Missy was right there and so was Ma. Then an unusually pretty woman got out of the truck and walked right up to Ma and gave her a big hug.

"I'm Mary Jane. It's so good to meet you. And you must be Missy."

They all exchanged hugs and grins for a while and then found their way into the house for coffee and yesterday's cinnamon rolls for dunking, the very thing that Sam loved most for breakfast.

It seemed that Sam had grown a couple inches and gained 50 pounds of muscle. He was a tough looking man with a quick smile. Wil was full of questions.

"We're here to stay Wil." said Sam. "We have to find a place to live until we can build something."

"You can stay here for now until we can get something figured out. And another thing, I know of a forty upstream a bit, hardly a quarter of a mile from here. They logged it a couple years ago, so you'd have to buy timber for the house, but that wouldn't be much of a problem." said Wil.

Sam looked over at Mary Jane and she seemed to think that it was a pretty good idea herself. They had saved a lot of money between them and had plenty for the house.

"The guys that went out to Montana with me are coming back here too, so we've got them and a few more to build the cabin. We'll need a pretty big one since we're just starting our family." said Sam. "We have the plans already drawn and these guys have built a good many buildings for me. Let's go look at that forty."

It was only 9:00 in the morning and the day had taken on a new course for Wil. They walked into the forty Wil talked about and Sam thought that the view was about as good as it gets. The place was covered with hundreds of birch trees and a few big red pines that were too big when they logged it over. All in all the place would make a fine home for them.

By the time they got back, Ma had already made a pan of caramel rolls and had them rising on the back of the cookstove. All the stuff from the truck was brought in and part of the living room was allocated to the Sam Anderson family. Sam and Mary Jane took the truck to the General Store and bought a new bed so even that was taken care of. By noon things were settled, and the land was purchased. An hour later, a deal had been made for the logs. Sam was a no- nonsense man and got right at the project.

At six that night as they were eating supper, another truck came into the yard. The rest of his crew from Montana had showed up and Tom Anderson was knocking on the door. Sam opened the door to find the whole crew there with lots of grins and laughing. They all agreed to come back the next day around noon to get started on the house, but for now they had an appointment at the local saloon.

The sun came up full and warm the next morning and Wil was watching it from his favorite spot, his bench overlooking the river. He looked up and there was Sam walking toward him, barefoot in the dew-wet grass with a big grin on his face.

"Guess we drank a few cups here before haven't we?" said Sam.

"We have indeed."

"It sure is good to be back home. When I left here, you told me that no matter which direction I went, it would always be uphill. It turned out that you were right. It was an up hill battle the whole way, but I made it to foreman in no time. Mr. Withers had faith in me and let me pretty much run things."

"Who?" said Wil.

"Mr. Withers, the man that owns the company."

Wil nearly fell off the bench.

"I got a feeling that I know that rascal. We was just kids together many years ago and we hunted and fished and chased up and down this river for miles. We grew up hard and lean and tougher that railroad spikes. I haven't seen him for a long time but here a couple days ago, I got a postcard from him saying that he'd be here to see me soon."

Sam told him all about the plan to start some new camps and how Mr. Withers wanted Wil to do the hiring. The whole thing took some getting used to, but Wil thought that he might take the job. The sun was starting to warm them a bit and it was time to get busy.

The process of building their new home was coming along nicely and the men worked until dark each day. By the third week, the well was put in and a small cistern pump was installed in the kitchen. None of the locals had such things as indoor privies so the word was spread about how the rich folks up-river had such a fine house. Then one day the new toilet and cast iron bathtub were delivered. These were installed by craftsmen from International Falls. All in all, the house was definitely one of a kind. The cookstove was one of the prettiest there was, with peach colored doors and side panels. It had two ovens and a warming oven on top. There was a very large hot water reservoir on the side as well. All of the money that they had saved was really coming in handy right now.

Moving in day was finally at hand and the whole family was there to help. Wil and Ma gave them a fine housewarming party with most of the local residents coming to wish them all well.

As Sam and Mary Jane were sitting eating a piece of cake, a man came and put his hand on Sam's shoulder.

"Congratulations Sam. You've got a fine home."

He turned around to see who was talking and nearly choked on his cake. It was Mr. Withers.

"Mr. Withers!" he exclaimed. "Where did you come from?"

"Just got in my boy. I had to see this piece of property I purchased. Now, where can I find Wil Morgan?"

Sam excused himself and led Mr. Withers out to the river bank where a few men had gathered around, sitting on stumps. He walked up behind Wil and pulled up a stump and sat next to him. The rest of the men nodded their heads at the new man and kept talking. Wil didn't look to see who it was.

"I guess they're opening as many as five new camps just south of Big Falls. They asked me to do the hiring." said Wil.

"And you better do a good job of it, too." said the man.

Wil, not used to such a threatening tone, turned quickly to see who was talking. His eyes tried to focus on the man sitting so close to him. Time had done its work and the man's voice had changed some, and the face had as well. Then he finally put it all together and a big grin covered Wil Morgan's face.

"Wilbur W. Withers. Damn it's been an awful long time."

Wil jumped to his feet at the same time as Mr. Withers did. They grabbed a fist full of handshake and then hugged each other fiercely. It had been a bucket full of years but the two men were still fast friends.

"Wilbur, what in the world brings you here?" asked Wil.

"Well, I'm the one that's opening them new camps you were just talking about. I bought some land by Big Falls and from what I heard, you will do the hiring to fill the place up. Sam's wife is in charge of the cook shacks and we're all going to make money. Now how does that sound?"

Wil looked around the circle of friends and said, "This rascal and I terrorized every critter for many miles when we was kids. We lived off the land here for a pile of summers and had a good time doing it. We trapped, hunted, fished, camped, told lies and made some darned good wine too."

Mr. Withers laughed hard and nodded in agreement. "We left no stone unturned. We did it all and more. The only problem was that I grew up and had to go to work one day or I'd still be here doing the very same things."

They walked down the road to Wil's cabin and walked inside.

"You know Wilbur, this very spot where the cabin sits is where you and I spent all those summers. When it came time to build, I didn't figure I could ever find a place I liked better. I'm 43 years old now and this summer, it's been 25 years since we were here."

"You old rascal, you look a little more gray, but you haven't changed much."

"Take off the bowler hat Wilbur. It makes you look to damned distinguished."

He took it off and Wil came to see the same young man he spent so much time with as a kid. He hadn't changed that much. He had a little pot belly and a bald spot on his head, but the twinkle was still there in his eyes.

"Did you ever get married?" asked Wil.

"Yup, I did. I think that I was about 23 then. We had a good life with plenty of money. We lived in New York pretty close to my folks place. My wife and I were expecting a baby and when it came time to deliver, she died in childbirth. There wasn't anything that we could do."

Wilbur choked up a bit.

"I left the city and everything I knew behind and headed into the mountains of Montana. I started a small logging business and been doing this ever since. I guess I made some money at it, but I did find that money wasn't worth a flip if you didn't pass it around to your friends. If you save it in a bank, it just gets dusty."

The two friends talked of old times for several hours. The laughing and joking around came back to them just like before.

"Tell me what you did with your life, Wil."

"Well, I found the prettiest woman in the whole world and talked her into marrying me. Now, that really took some talking I'll tell ya. An old jackpine savage like me isn't real appealing to a gal like that, but she must have believed there was something good underneath all those whiskers. We farmed for a while in southern Minnesota and had twin boys. They died in an accident though."

Wil got a pained look on his face. It seemed that both of them had some bad times.

"Other than that, I cut timber, farmed, trap and hunt for a living. We never got rich, but we never wanted that either. I guess the most important thing is that we are quite happy here on the river. Life can be a bit tough, but we manage. Now we got another youngster that's quite a handful. I thought I was too old to have more kids, but Ma showed me I was wrong once again."

The two spent quite a bit of time drinking coffee and reminiscing. The fire of their youth was rekindled and a hunting trip was planned for ducks up on Hay Creek for the fall. It had indeed been quite a while.

"Well my friend, it's time for me to hit the road. First I have to talk to my foreman Sam. Then I'm going up to Big falls. I plan on heading back to the Bad Mountain Camp on Monday, so I have a lot to do before then."

The two walked back outside and over to Sam and Mary Jane's house. The crowd had thinned some and it was just a couple of groups left; one for the men and one for women. Sam and Mr. Withers found a quiet spot and discussed business for quite a while. Then they broke off their discussion and each headed in a different direction. Sam now had a big job ahead of him.

The next day, Sam headed up to Big Falls to meet Mr. Withers. They drove for several hours and did quite a bit of hiking through the woods. By nightfall, they had a pretty good idea where the camps would be built, but mainly they knew where the first one would be. Sam already had his crew hired for the construction of the camp. They would hire a couple teams of horses and teamsters right away to clear land near the river for the camp. Sam planned on driving there each day from his house on the river with the trip only being 35 miles. The rest of the men would stay there in tents.

Construction began with the bunkhouse. It took the best part of two weeks and then the men didn't have to stay in tents any longer. From there, it was a cook shack and that took quite a long time to build. The crew had to fend for themselves and each man took a turn at cooking.

Late one afternoon as the men were peeling logs, a man walked up to them and asked for a job. Nobody there had the authority to hire so they told him to come back in the morning when Sam was there.

The next morning while Sam and the crew were finishing up peeling the logs, a man walked up behind Sam and said he was looking for a job. Sam turned around to look at the man and the fire of recognition burned brightly once again in his mind. Here was the man in the canoe, the man who killed his family, the man who tried to kill Wil, the man he wanted dead. He instantly grabbed him by the arm and spun him to the ground. He stood over the greasy haired man and rage threatened to overtake him.

"You bastard, you're the one who killed my folks!" And with that, he kicked the man hard in the ribs.

"Get up you bastard or I'll kill you right where you are."

It was Scooter all right, but he not only was a killer, he was a survivor too. Again Sam kicked him in the ribs.

"Get up Scooter or so help me, I'll kill you right there on the ground."

Scooter knew he was in bad trouble now with the whole group of six men gathered around him. He quickly rolled out of the way and came up with a pistol in his hand. He aimed at Sam and pulled the trigger. The man hit his mark and Sam doubled over in pain. By the time the smoke cleared, Scooter was nowhere to be seen. Sam was lying on the ground in a pool of his own blood.

Tom Anderson kneeled down by Sam and lifted his shirt. The bullet hit Sam in the stomach at an angle and went out his left side. The men bandaged him up and got him into the back of the truck.

They headed to the International Falls Hospital, less than 30 miles away. It didn't look too good for Sam. His face had lost all of its color and he was having a hard time breathing. He was a tough man but a bullet in the stomach was usually fatal to anyone.

The trip there seemed to go by pretty slowly. Sam was bleeding from his mouth and having a hard time getting any air. His skin was cold and his eyes fluttered once in a while. Coming through town, they just kept blowing the horn so folks would let them through.

They carried him inside and the doctor and nurses took him away. Tom Anderson stayed there with Sam and the rest of the men got back into the truck and headed south to tell his wife.

In a short time, the Sheriff was at the hospital talking to Tom. He wanted to know who had shot Sam and all Tom knew was that Sam called him Scooter. The Sheriff knew from that who to look for, but this was no easy case. He had killed a lot of good people and had been hard to catch up with. The man knew the woods and stayed hidden until he was forced by hunger to look for a job or kill again for food. Now he had a good idea of where to look.

The Sheriff formed a posse and a crew of 25 men on horseback combed the area for two days but again came up empty.

Sam spent a long time in the hospital and it took nearly a week before the doctor said that he thought he was going to recover. If Sam hadn't been such a tough man, he never would have survived. He ate an inordinate amount of chicken broth and within three weeks, came out of the hospital, a bit worse for wear. He spent a couple more weeks eating Mary Jane's good home cooking and then it was back to work.

During all of his time healing, he thought about the Scooter's face. He could still see him holding that gun and that cloud of gun smoke. Sam knew guns well, and knew it was Wil's .45 Colt that shot him. He still had the same job to do as when he was a kid and it wasn't going to go away. Scooter could evade the law at will so it was going to be up to Sam to get the job done.

The killer had read in the paper the story of Sam nearly being killed. He had faced Sam head-on and both men knew that it wouldn't be the last time.

# CHAPTER 9
## FALL ON THE BIGFORK

Midsummer found Missy Anderson and Peter Davis together much more than usual. Peter was out of work for the summer like Missy, and spent a lot of time helping Wil with farming. He was adept at handling livestock and all he needed was for Missy to smile at him once in a while and a little food to keep his strength up. He had grown to be deeply in love with Missy and considering the fact that she couldn't talk he knew how she felt about him, too.

The camp that Missy and Peter worked at, had gotten to the point that they had to travel too far to get to the timber. So that meant either closing down the operation or moving camp. The owners let out the word that they would be discontinuing operations permanently. While that was a bit of bad news for them, it did give them some time to explore other things to do for a living.

One Sunday morning, the whole family gathered at Sam and Mary Jane's for breakfast and talk. The closing of the camp was the topic of conversation for the morning and Wil asked Peter if he'd like to come to work for the new "Gut and Liver Camp"? They needed a pencil pusher with some experience. Peter jumped at the chance. Missy beamed from ear to ear.

Then it was Mary Jane's turn.

"I've been looking for a head cook at the new camp and from what I've seen, you sure do have the experience Missy. What do you think?"

Missy beamed with pride and nodded yes. The most important job in the new camp was filled and Mary Jane had a load off her mind. Filling this position had been a hard thing for her since she knew almost nobody in the area. With her hiring, that also meant that Wil's job would be made easier. A lot of the jacks would follow a good cook and she hoped that this would be the case.

Wil and Ma seemed to be a bit busier than usual with the new baby. He wanted to be held a lot and that meant that Ma couldn't do a lot of the chores she normally did. Missy and Peter took over as much as possible, but when it came to cooking, Wil insisted that his wife make his meals. He loved the things she made for him and couldn't get used to anyone else's cooking.

The baby awoke in the middle of the night in late summer crying in a way that meant pain. It was more of a scream. His little belly was puffed out and hard as a rock. She gave him peppermint water mixed with sugar and that seemed to comfort him for a while, but by morning, they had Sam take them to International Falls to see the doctor. The diagnosis was unclear but it felt to the doctor that the baby had some kind of a tumor growing inside his lower chest. He needed an operation and that cost a lot of money.

Ma and Wil sat in the waiting room waiting for the doctor to come out and talk to them. Ma was rocking the now screaming baby and trying her best to comfort him. When the doctor finally came out, he sat between them and gave them the bad news. He was pretty sure that it was a tumor but he wasn't sure about his skills with a baby that small. The other part that scared him was what effect the ether might have on him. With a baby that small, they were never sure what the ether might do. The major problem was that if they tried to take the baby to another hospital in Minneapolis, he'd probably die on the way there. Time was against them. He asked them to talk it over for a few minutes and he'd come back to see what they wanted to do.

"If we try to get him to the city, he'll die on the way." said Wil.

"And if we have them operate on him here, we might lose him." said Ma. "Seems that we better have the doc do it right here. Let's pray Wil."

So in the little white waiting room, Ma and Wil asked for wisdom in making this most difficult of decisions. They raised their heads when they heard the doc walk back in and knew that it had to be done right here and right now. Ma handed the baby to the doctor.

Within the hour, the child was in the operating room breathing ether and the doctor was making an incision in the child's abdomen. It was clear to him right away that it was indeed a tumor. He worked on freeing up the mass for quite some time and then it was time to close. The operation had been a success and the child would be fine. The tumor was almost eight ounces and had been growing at such a rate that if not for the surgery he would have died within a very short time. These were trying times for Wil and Ma and they kept a vigil over their child night and day as he healed. No cause was ever determined but the little boy was allowed to go home in a few days.

Missy and Peter were being a bit more open about showing their affection for each other and one afternoon while Wil was sitting in the shade out by the river, Peter came up to him and sat down on the bench.

"Mr. Morgan. I'd like to marry Missy and you seem to be the one to ask since her folks are gone. I'll take good care of her and make sure nobody ever hurts her."

Wil sat there for a bit, not quite knowing what to say. He had been looking after Missy since she was a little kid.

"What are your plans for work Peter?"

"Well, I do want to stay on as the pencil pusher, but I want to be a preacher someday, too. Maybe I can do both if I work hard at it."

"Sounds pretty good to me Peter. Have you discussed marriage with Missy?" asked Wil.

"No. I wanted to get your permission first. That's the right way to do things."

"Thanks, Peter. You're a good man. Now, if you can convince

Missy of that, you might just stand a chance. Give it a try, boy. You'd make a good addition to our little family."

Peter blushed some and said that he'd get busy trying to win her over.

In a period of three days, Peter had an announcement at supper one night.

"Wil and Ma, Missy and I are going to get married this fall. We wanted you to be the first to know."

Missy beamed, Ma cried, Wil walked outside and Peter was left wondering if they were happy or sad about the idea. Then Ma started to laugh. She was a bit overwhelmed right then and was quite happy about it. After the wedding they would move up to the new camp and that would be their home for the winter.

Summer was turning into fall and the colors on the river took on a regal splendor. Everywhere you looked, there were patches of red and gold. In the early fall sunshine, the river too looked prettier than ever. Mr Withers, good to his word, showed up one night to see if Wil was ready to go duck hunting on Saturday morning, the opening of hunting season. He was indeed, and Friday night, the old friends loaded decoys, guns and supplies and headed downriver to Hay creek. From there they went over five beaver dams and into the Lost Forty area. Wil and he had camped here many times and it was like coming home for them both.

The supplies were all unloaded and the canoe turned upside down for the night. Within a few minutes, Wil had a good fire going, boiling some of the dark water of the creek. They had learned when quite young to boil the heck out of the water or get really sick. It made wonderful coffee.

"It's been a long time since I had coffee this good Wil. I sure have missed a lot of years here haven't I."

The smoke from their small campfire arose from the glow and disappeared upwards into the inky darkness.

"Yup. I thought about you every year, wondering where you were."

They sipped their coffee together in the light of the small campfire. Out on Hay Creek they could hear a mallard once in a while and the sound of geese flying over in the night sky. Then as they sat there talking, the sky cleared of clouds revealing a wall of light way off somewhere to the north. The northern lights were putting on a spectacular show just for them. The lights would swing and sway back and forth. Then they would dim and nearly quit only to flash brightly and start to move again. The colors changed into soft blues and pinks. Two old friends, reunited after such a long time sat watching the Creator's handiwork.

"What did you bring for supper Wil?"

"Now where did you get the idea that I brought anything?"

"Well, with that woman of yours being such a good cook and the fact that you probably weigh 20 pounds more than when we were kids, I kinda figured that you brought something."

"Well, we just butchered, so I brought a pair of T-Bone steaks about a pound each. I also brought a loaf of fresh bread and some potatoes. Then for the final item, I brought a large jar of horseradish. You take care of the potatoes like you used to when we were kids."

Wilbur took down the frying pan and threw in a couple of strips of bacon. Then while they were cooking, he went to the creek and washed up a couple of big potatoes. Then he cut up a small onion. He threw it all into the pan with the bacon and sat back enjoying the smells he had missed for so long. Wil got the big pan hot and threw in the steaks. They sizzled and popped and then settled down to some serious frying. After a short while, Wil flipped them over and asked how long before the taters would be done. It looked like they would be finished at about the same time.

Wil made up a couple of plates with their creations and topped the whole thing off with a big dose of horseradish. This was a meal fit for a king. The two ate in silence for quite a while. Then Wilbur stood and declared the meal to be the finest he had ever eaten.

"You make any money at logging Wilbur?"

"Wil, I make so much money that I'm having trouble finding a place to hide it!" He laughed for a bit. "You know Wil, I really do make a lot of money but I have nobody to leave it to. That means that when I die, it will all go to the state and that is a bad thought. So I pay high wages to my men so I can spread the wealth around. I always want to keep a half million for myself and I've done that for a long time, but the rest I spend on people. I get a lot of satisfaction doing that."

"Why don't you get married again?"

"Well, I thought about it once, but now I'm getting a bit stuck in my ways. I might though, if the right one comes along."

"I think I'm about ready to hit the sack," said Wil. "It's been quite a day."

And with that, Wil turned and went inside the tent.

Wil was the first one awake as usual and had the pot of coffee going. Wilbur came out of the tent shivering from the cold.

"I don't think I've ever been so cold before."

"You got soft Wilbur. Used to be that you slept under the canoe with no blankets."

"I guess you're right Wil. I'm used to sleeping in a fancy bed with a goose down quilt."

They got their coffee down and started to get their guns ready for the hunt. Once in the canoe, Wilbur paddled hard like he did when he was a kid. They put out their decoys in the near darkness and settled down on a beaver lodge. As it got closer to getting light, they could see big flocks of mallards off in the distance near the main river, but none near them. Then one at a time, wood ducks started to show up. The first shot was taken by Wilbur and he downed a beautiful drake. Then Wil got one. There were no mallards to shoot at, but the wood ducks and blue winged teal gave them quite a bit of shooting. After a couple of hours, the shooting stopped completely and they went back to camp to get things ready for the trip back home.

Wilbur only had one day and he made the best of it. On the return trip, he sat in front and shot several mallards. He was having a great hunt and that pleased Wil.

Missy and Peter had decided to get married at Wil and Ma's place on the river and the event had the makings for a big celebration. On the big day, people came from everywhere. Peter's parents came from Grand Rapids along with many cousins. On Missy's side, there was everyone from the whole community. Everyone knew that she had lost her parents, but they felt like she was their own. Even Mr. Withers was there for the big event.

At the right time, the preacher showed up and took charge of everything. Missy was wearing a beautiful white dress that Ma had made. She had a veil and pink flowers in her hand. Peter wore a black suit with shiny black shoes.

"Now you two stand right here in front of me," said the preacher. "Now, Ma and Wil, I want you to stand behind Missy. Now, on this side, I want Peter's folks to stand behind him. There. Now all the rest of you fill in behind everyone else."

So the whole community, plus some, stood behind the couple and waited for the preacher to start the service. He made a nice speech about the holiness of marriage and how God blesses each marriage as if it were made in heaven. Then it came time for the vows. Peter was shaking like he had the chills.

"Do you Missy Anderson take Peter to be your husband, to have and to hold from this day forth, for richer and poorer, in sickness and in health 'til death you do part?"

Missy nodded her head and the preacher acknowledged it. Then it was Peter's turn. He heard some of the words, but not many, and then said "Yes".

Then before he knew what hit him, it was over and the crowd was cheering. He and Missy were married, it was done and he had survived. He was red as a beet and all at once the color left his face and he tipped over on the grass. The strain had been too much for him. Missy sat down on the grass by her now passed out husband and wiped his face with a cool wet cloth. His eyes fluttered open.

"What happened?" he asked.

The whole crowd laughed and cheered. It was done and they had survived, albeit a bit worse for wear. The community never forgot the wedding and the way Peter tipped over. Each wedding for quite some time was preceded by, "Now don't pass out like Peter Davis."

The construction of the new camp was coming to an end. The cook shack, two bunkhouses, four large outhouses, a small blacksmith's shop, a storehouse and office for Peter and a large livestock shed were all nearly completed. Sam had found several teams of oxen and horses to move the logs and the place was starting to look like a working camp.

Missy had her work cut out for her as well. She had a supply list that was several pages long. She gave the job of filling the order to her first cookie. He would have to either go to International Falls or down to Minneapolis for this. She was only cooking for a few men now, so it gave her some time to get ready for all of the men that would show up in a month.

Quite a few of the lumberjacks were put to work putting up firewood for the camp. Sam figured that he needed around 40 cords, all split and stacked and that took a few days to accomplish. A couple of men were already run off for not pulling their share of the load. It was better to get rid of them early.

Sam was overseeing the remainder of the camp and at times the healing gunshot wound slowed him up some. He had purchased a water wagon for icing the trails to the river and that was due in today. The only way that they could get the logs to the river was to ice the trails for the teams to pull on and then it had to be on a downhill grade if it were to move at all. Then there was the problem of getting the load stopped once it got moving. That is where the experience of good teamsters came in. If it got moving too fast, the load would end up killing the team and perhaps the teamster as well, so the method of an emergency stop was to throw a hand full of sand in front of the runners.

The temperature had been dropping pretty hard by mid November and the word was spread that operations would begin on November 20th. Lumberjacks came from everywhere and hiring was done by Wil as he saw fit. He knew most of the men because he had worked with them. A few tried to get their first job with Wil, but he wanted experienced men and wouldn't take less.

Supper the first night was a bit better than what they would usually get. It was a get acquainted meal so the men would know what the meals were like. Missy had roasted a quarter of beef and sliced it thinly, putting steaming plates of meat on the tables. There were bowls of boiled potatoes and large amounts of gravy. Carrots in brown sugar glaze and fresh bread adorned the tables. As a final reward for signing on with the Gut and Liver, Missy produced large bowls of bread pudding with raisins and walnuts. Many big pots of hot coffee topped off the meal. It was still like other camps though, when it came to talking. Shut up, eat up and get out. As the men were leaving the cook shack, they all thanked Missy.

The sawyer over in the saw filer's shack was putting the final edge on the six foot saws. The cutters and rakers were like razors. During the course of the day, the men would touch up the saws, but they darned well better know what they were doing or feel the wrath of the little saw filer. He was a perfectionist in his own way and didn't want his saws ruined by an amateur.

In the bunkhouse, the men were all settled into their new straw beds. They had strung many wire lines to be used for drying their socks. Snort-boards separated the double bunked men.

There was a large wood stove on each end of the shack so the trick of surviving the winter was to get a spot that was warm enough to survive the forty below nights, but not so close to the stove that you spent the night sweating.

The first morning of operations had the men excited and ready to get working. The cookie blew the horn and the stampede was on. There were great bowls of stewed prunes, oatmeal, cream and sugar. This was what the men needed to carry them to lunchtime. They ate fast and paired up for the day.

The weather that first morning was bitter cold, but the men were dressed for it. The temperature was around 30 below and once in a while, they would hear what sounded like a pistol shot. They all knew that it was the trees popping from the cold. The moisture inside the trees would expand and the tree would make a loud noise as it split.

Sam gathered them all together outside the cook shack and the sky pilot Peter said a few words of encouragement and asked a blessing on the men to keep them safe. The first day's logging in the Gut and Liver was about to begin. Sam had the areas marked out on a map for the men so they headed out as the sun peeked over a distant hill.

It was a race. A number of the men had placed bets who would get to yell "timber" first. It was only a matter of a few minutes and it came with the accompanying sound of a big red pine crashing to the ground. From there on, it was a steady sound of the big saws cutting pine.

A short time later, a crew yelled for a team of horses and a dray. The big logs were rolled up onto the dray using rails hooked to the sides of the dray in an incline. The first ones loaded easily, but by the time the load started to get higher, it took a lot of work to get them to the top of the pile. A pile 12 feet high was nothing unusual. Then with a whistle and shout the team leaned into their load and ever so slowly it started to move toward the river and eventually in the spring toward the big mills.

Missy and the Cookies had been working hard all morning getting the lunch ready for the men. There was an awful pile of sandwiches from last nights roast beef and many gallons of coffee.

It was only 11:15 and they still had 45 minutes until they took the men their noon meal. Missy motioned for all the help to sit down for a while and relax. The busiest part of the day was done. After lunch it was a bit slower pace. The men didn't eat until 6 p.m. so that gave them time to be a bit more creative.

Missy came out from the back store room and sat down to make out the evenings menu.

Italian Spaghetti and Meatballs

Garlic toast

Apple Pie

Coffee or tea.

She doubted that many of the men had eaten spaghetti, but they better get used to it. She was a wonderful cook and when Mary Jane checked on her, she could offer little in the way of improvement.

With operations going well in the Gut and Liver, Sam decided to start the second camp. He would need his usual crew of men. Tom Anderson was put in charge of the job and within the first two weeks, they had a bunkhouse done. He ruled with an iron fist and a big grin. Seemed that everyone really liked and respected him.

One evening, Wil and Ma had Sam and Mary Jane as guests for dinner. Ma had made fried beef steak for supper and Wil loved it, using large amounts of the always present horseradish. Then for dessert, she had made a big Rhubarb pie. They all enjoyed the meal greatly.

Sam and Wil were sitting by the fireplace after supper.

"We got to think of a name for the new camp." said Sam. "I been scratching my head for days over this one."

"I never been much good at that stuff so don't look at me," he laughed.

Ma walked up to Sam and said that she had it all figured out.

"How about the Rhubarb and Horseradish Camp?" she asked grinning.

With that, the new camp was affectionately called the R&H Timber Camp.

The duties that Missy had taken on in the camp were starting to get the best of her. Some of her cookies were slacking off and leaving more work for her than they should. She was a small woman and the help was trying her patience. When she noticed a job left undone, she grabbed the cookie by the arm and took them to the job, pointing at it and smiling. This only lasted for a short while and then it was time for harsher measures.

One morning after breakfast, Missy noticed that some of the dishes were left undone from the night before. She knew who the offender was and it was the same one as from several times before. She walked back into her room and sat down at her desk. She took out a sheet of paper and tore it in half. Then with pen and ink wrote, "You're fired. Go to Peter and draw your pay." Then she walked back into the kitchen and handed the note to the ex-cookie. He looked at it and his face got red with anger.

Peter and a peddler were sitting in the corner discussing an order when they heard a slight ruckus. They looked up in time to see one of the cookies grab Missy's arm and push her backward into the stove.

She tried to catch herself, but her hand landed on the griddle with a sickening sizzling sound. She grabbed for her hand, and the man pushed her again. Peter gave out a loud yell and was on the man in an instant. His first punch landed on the back of the man's head and the second caught him dead on the nose. He fell backward on the floor and then got up to fight. He grabbed a large knife from the counter and took a big swing at Peter, making him fall backwards to keep from getting cut. The man's intense anger made him a ferocious enemy. He kept coming at Peter and it looked like he was going to cut him or worse, kill him.

Peter rolled under a table but the man was right there after him, stabbing thin air. Peter kicked at the man's leg trying to knock him over but that only made the man aim at his leg. Then Peter thought to roll over and over under several tables. He was at last free from the knife and had time to draw his Colt.

"Now, that's about as far as you're going today," he said with the gun aimed right at the man's heart.

The ex-cookie stopped for only a second and then leaped right at Peter, the knife leading the way. Peter hesitated for a moment and the room filled with smoke. The cookie crumpled and lay dead on the floor with the knife still in his hand. It was the worst thing that could ever happen to a young man. He had killed someone in a fight to protect Missy. She was burned badly, but knew to put her hand in the snow right away to lessen the burn.

Peter sent for the Sheriff and within a couple of hours, he was there to load the body. No charges would be filed against Peter, but he did want to know why he was carrying a Colt .45.

"That business with Scooter still has Missy pretty scared and if he ever comes for her, I want to be ready."

"Well, make darned sure you kill him on your first shot. You won't get a second chance." said the Sheriff.

"Remember Sheriff, she's the one that saw him murder that jack in the cook shack."

The next few days had Peter doing some serious soul searching about killing the cookie. His religion had taught him not to kill and it was part of his life to obey that commandment. His other choice would have been to take a chance with the man. He had a kind of crazy look in his eye that said he meant business. For his age, Peter had seen a lot, but never a killing. It seemed that something went off inside him when he saw his wife in trouble.

The following Sunday had Peter standing in front of the bunkhouse as sky pilot. He preached a short sermon and then apologized to the men for killing the cookie. Any way you looked at it, Peter had killed one of them and he felt a great amount of guilt for taking the man's life.

After the sermon was done, several men came up to Peter and told him that he had done the right thing. They all really loved Missy and quite probably would have done the same thing themselves. That put it to rest with Peter and allowed him to get on with his life.

# CHAPTER 10
## SCOOTER

Survival was at the core of this man Scooter, this most vicious of murderers. He was like a most serious predator. What he wanted he took.

Life for Scooter had turned a bit for the worse and getting enough food to keep him alive was getting to be a problem. He robbed traps from the whole area and had the trappers up in arms as to who it was. He could take the fur, but he couldn't go to town to sell it. He ate the beaver and muskrats and threw the hides away, the opposite of most trappers.

He began his life of crime while a young man when his father had him help on some of his trips to Winnipeg. They robbed a bank and shot the teller. There seemed to be no limits on his father and as such, he also had no limits.

Sometimes in the middle of the night, he tried to remember his mother but he wasn't sure that he even had one. He remembered a sister that cooked meals for them sometimes, but she ran off with a trapper when she was twelve. Her life in the bush of Canada was hard and she took her first opportunity to leave her family, never looking back. Other than these sparse memories, there was no good in his life. He endured many whippings from his always drunken father and learned that violence of any form was part of living.

By the time Scooter turned ten, he was drinking whiskey right along with his father. There were women that he brought in for a season or two, but nothing permanent. Then they all just disappeared, silently, quickly, permanently and always after some kind of an argument. He remembered seeing his father beat them and learned the lessons well.

One night in a drunken rage, his father tried to beat him and he fought back. He was very drunk from the cheap whiskey he bought at the fort and when he hit Scooter, he nearly knocked him unconscious. He was bleeding badly from a cut on his head but the anger was building, bubbling to the surface and when he came up off the floor, he grabbed a chunk of firewood and beat the old man to death. His rage burned like a torch and even after the deed was done, he still smoldered for many hours. At last, he was free of the dominance of his father and from here on he would call the shots.

The next morning Scooter dragged the body of his father down to the lake. He put the body in the small boat and rowed out to the middle. Then with little thought as to what he had done, tied rocks to his legs and dumped him into the dark cold water of Lake Harriet.

A few weeks later, he went to town and reported the disappearance of his father. The Mounties thought this to be a bit strange because the man had been on many trips that lasted weeks. Why was this short time any different? And so Scooter's life of crime started in grand fashion. Now he would make his own decisions.

Life was getting hard for him on his own. He had no skills and had only gone through the fourth grade in Canada. He tried to get work on farms during the wheat harvest, but usually didn't last too long because of his temper. He had cut a man near Saskatoon in a bar fight and by the age of 30 had made a bad name for himself.

When he was barely into his 30's, he murdered a man for whatever he had in his pockets. He had been riding the rails looking for work and found himself in a rocking empty boxcar with an old hobo. While the man slept, Scooter took a small piece of rope and choked the man to death. This in itself wasn't so unusual, but the fact that he was grinning as the man struggled for his last breath told a lot about him. He had absolutely no regard for life.

After going through his pockets, he opened the door of the boxcar and unceremoniously dumped the body of the old hobo out along the tracks. There was little chance that anyone would ever find the man.

He continued to ride the rails finding the pickings a bit easier. Any man found alone was in serious trouble. In the hobo jungles, small camps made near the tracks, the men could usually find the makings for a large pot of soup. They would go through the nearby towns stealing or begging for anything that they could put in the pot. Usually, a full belly meant that nobody would get killed that night. These were tough times for a lot of men, and the ones that survived got tougher or died, some at the hands of Scooter.

He eventually found his way to the lumber camps of Montana, but it seemed that his temper always got him in trouble. One morning he was eating breakfast in the cook shack, when another lumberjack of equally bad temper took offense at something and beat Scooter nearly to death. He never said much to anyone, but the next payday he purchased a small knife to carry in his right boot.

The man that beat him was still in camp and Scooter's rage grew each time he saw the man. He wanted revenge and was going to get it in any form.

In the dark of the night, Scooter was walking around the camp when he saw this most hated man walking toward him. He stepped behind a tree and waited for the man to come to him. As he went by, Scooter stepped out and stuck his knife in the man's back. As he hit the ground, Scooter was on him and stabbed him several more times, finishing the job. Then he ran into the woods to spend the rest of the night. When the cooks horn blew next morning, he joined the crowd and went inside to eat his breakfast.

In a short time he heard some noise outside and assumed that the body had been found.

The Sheriff questioned a lot of men and heard about the beating that Scooter had been given at the hands of the now dead man. With no evidence, the Sheriff filed the case unsolved.

There was no doubt in the minds of the entire camp who had

killed that lumberjack so life got a bit tough for Scooter. They watched him like a hawk and the men stayed in pairs for safety. The foreman eventually fired him and the whole camp breathed a sigh of relief. He moved on down the road a few miles and got another job. A lumberjacks bad name usually followed him for a lifetime, but he was smart enough to change his name with each job.

His appearance was that of a man that didn't care for himself. His hair was long, dirty and black. And he had a slight crook in his nose from some previous altercation. His clothes were rarely clean and his hands were heavily calloused from swinging an axe.

He never seemed to last long at any job. He had a bad temper and the look of a man that could do nearly anything. He never made friends since they would eventually get in his way.

One camp he worked at in Minnesota was paying a bit more than the usual so Scooter was making an attempt to stay out of trouble. On payday a few of the men took an old cracker barrel and covered the top with a green woolen blanket. A poker game started that had the makings of being high stakes. Scooter and another man formed an alliance to take a couple men to the cleaners. When Scooter got a good hand, he'd wink at the other man and then they would start raising the stakes. The victim would have no idea what was happening and soon would be cleaned out.

Scooter had spent a lot of time alone playing with a deck of cards. He could palm an ace or put one up his sleeve with no difficulty. On the next night after payday, the stakes got some higher and the men that won the night before continued in a higher stakes game. Scooter and his confederate were still in the running.

Les Anderson wasn't a man to give away his money. He saved everything for his family. He was sitting on the edge of his bunk watching the card game and a friend of his was getting taken to the cleaners once again. As he watched, from his angle he saw Scooter slip an ace inside his shirt. Then at the appropriate time, he switched the ace for another card and that gave him a winning hand. The pot was large and his friend was wiped out.

Les yelled from his bunk that Scooter cheated and that brought a hush to the room. He jumped from his bunk and ripped open Scooter's shirt revealing the card. Scooter grabbed his boot knife and Les saw it coming. He hit Scooter a couple times and that was the end of the card game.

A couple men dragged Scooter out of the bunk house and into the snow. They took his money and left him to wake up or freeze.

Les Anderson had made a seriously bad enemy that night, one that would follow him to the very ends of the earth for his revenge. Les knew how bad Scooter was, and did his best to stay away from him.

Scooter was always on the lookout for a way to get at Les but the opportunity never came. Spring breakup meant that everyone was let go for the season except for the river pigs. Les headed back to his home on the river to do some farming and see his family. Scooter knew where Les lived and at night he would paddle by his cabin on the Bigfork River plotting his revenge.

It was mid summer and Scooter figured that he had waited long enough to get even. He paddled down river in the dark, pulling his canoe up a couple hundred yards from the cabin. As near as he could figure it was after midnight. He had made a fire bomb out of a half gallon whiskey jug filled with coal oil. He stuffed a rag into the bottle and turned it upside down to wet the wick.

Very quietly he moved near the side window of the cabin. In the darkness a flame sparked and grew illuminating this face of hate and evil. It joined the oil soaked rag and then grew brighter. Then for a short moment in time, Scooter hesitated, not sure he wanted to do in the whole family. Then his sworn anger at Les Anderson took over and he threw the fire bomb with all of his strength through the window.

There was a scream and Scooter was headed for his canoe, running hard. He jumped in and paddled furiously to get out of the area. This coward of a man was now grinning broadly as he paddled in the darkness. He had gotten his revenge from Les Anderson.

Such was the life of a murderer, Brad "Scooter" Sherman.

Wil had done most of the hiring that needed to be done so far and

Mr. Withers, true to his word, paid Wil a great sum of money. He hadn't seen this much cash in his life and he felt like a rich man. Cash money was always in short supply. It would be quite some time until they would need to fill the third camp. He was settling back into his routine on the river.

February was half over and the camps were producing many cords of good red pine. There had been no more trouble for a few weeks. Missy was doing a good job for the camp and the men all looked after her. Peter was getting to be quite a preacher and the folks in town one week asked him to preach a sermon at the Lutheran Church. The thought that the townspeople liked him made him feel good.

Missy and Peter came to dinner one Sunday to Wil and Ma's place on the river. After the dinner was eaten, the men retired to the chairs by the fireplace, discussing everything from saws to sausage.

The other ladies were sitting at the table doing some sewing. Missy had been having some trouble keeping her food down and the smells of some of the things she cooked, made her pretty sick. Peter walked over to the kitchen table and asked Ma if she thought Missy was alright. He was pretty concerned about her getting sick so often. With Missy still not being able to talk, Ma started to question her about many things and soon asked Peter to go back and sit with Wil.

After a short while, Ma came to the conclusion that Missy was pregnant. There was no fooling her and in a while she asked Peter to again come sit down with them.

"Have you ever wanted any children Peter?" Ma asked.

"You bet we do. But sometimes it takes quite a while to make a family." said Peter.

Missy was grinning broadly and Peter didn't see what was so funny.

"When would you like to start this family?"

"Well, as soon as I can get a good job, and we can afford it."

Peter looked around the table and saw that everyone there was grinning except for him. Then it dawned on him what she was saying.

"Missy? Are you?" Peter asked.

She grinned at him and nodded her head and then went over and sat on his lap. She wrapped her arms around him and kissed his cheek. Then Peter knew that he was indeed going to be a father. This was the biggest day in his life. Missy was beaming and the couple sat there, each thinking about the new life growing inside Missy.

Ma and Wil were pretty happy as well. Wil had hoped for a Grandson but he decided that either a boy or girl would be fine with him.

It didn't take long for the word to get out at the camp. Missy had offers of help from a lot of people. The old jacks that hadn't smiled or said a kind word in years grinned at Missy and offered her any help she might need. It did seem that the whole camp had adopted her.

Wil wasn't as hard pressed as usual to earn money in the winter so he went back to trapping as he had when he was younger. This was one of his favorite things and the thrill of checking his sets every other day hadn't changed. Sometimes when the snow was deep, he would have to use trail shoes to stay on top of the crust. This cut down on the number of miles he could make, but he still had seventy traps to cover every other day.

Early one morning he left home heading south toward the big swamp. He hadn't been there for several years and he remembered that the trapping used to be pretty good. He carried a Duluth pack nearly full of traps and the weight at first really wore him down. He had traveled nearly four miles from home before he started to make sets. He was after nearly anything that had fur.

He noticed some fisher tracks and what appeared to be those of a cougar. He made a couple sets and moved on up a stream looking for otter. In another mile, he had several more sets that he thought looked pretty good. He left the stream and headed into the big pines. There he saw a different story. Pine martin tracks were spread around liberally and this got his attention. The whole area looked like it hadn't been trapped in many years.

His course led him back toward the cabin and by the end of daylight, he was nearing the river. He stopped in the shed and took off his snowshoes. The Duluth pack was once again empty and he hung it back in it's place.

He walked in just in time for supper. Ma looked at him and told him to wash up for supper. He didn't have to be asked twice. The baby was sitting at the table in his highchair trying to get to the mashed potatoes and Ma hurried Wil up some saying that the poor child was starving there right in front of them and she laughed.

"How did that new area look Wil?" Ma asked.

"Not too bad from first look. I saw tracks from a cougar and a lot of fisher tracks. Good cash money from those I'd guess."

"I think your little helper here might like to give trapping a try. Do you want to take him along next time you go?"

"Might just be a while before he can do that, but the way he gets around now makes me think it won't be too long."

"Where did you go today?" asked Ma.

I went south into that big swamp and followed the stream for a while. Sure is pretty back there. There's a lot of big pine.

The next day he spent trapping muskrats near the house. On the following day he was up early getting his breakfast ready. He had coffee and toast for breakfast and threw a couple biscuits in his pocket in case he got hungry.

He strapped on his Colt 45 and went to the shed to get his Duluth pack. This time it was empty and the going much easier in spite of the six inches of new snow. At his first set, he could see from quite a way off that there was nothing in the trap. Then he went on for nearly a mile when he found a big fisher in a trap. He clubbed it to death and picked up the trap to be reset later. From the swamp he again went up the small stream and the next three sets had otter in them. At this rate, he was making money.

By early afternoon he was in the big pines and picked up a martin to finish off the day. As he rounded the pines headed for home, he saw a set of human tracks heading south. He wondered who would be going in that direction.

A couple days later, he was on his trapline and early on found that someone had robbed one of his traps. They had taken a martin and left the trap there. Then he noticed that the thief was following his trail checking each of Wil's traps. The man wore moccasins, like his friends the Ojibwe. He was somewhat perplexed because he had never had any trouble with the Indians. He counted them all as his friends.

The days trapping gave up very little and he decided that the next time he went out, he'd pull his traps and go somewhere else.

Early that day, he was on the trail way before sunup. At 3:00 a.m. it was almost like daylight with the moon casting long shadows on the snow. The silence was amazing as he listened to his racing heartbeat. When he stopped to catch his breath he heard the call of a wolf a long way to the east. He loved the sights and sounds of his world.

As he stood there, he saw the figure of a man on his trail behind him. The man was moving from tree to tree silently, trying to catch up to him. He wondered who would be out in the cold so early in the morning and why.

Wil decided to move into the brush close by and then backtrack to get a look at who was following him. He got down in the snow and covered himself partially. The man came right by Wil and he saw that he was carrying a 30-30. Wil jumped up with his hand on his gun. Scooter went to raise the rifle and saw right away that he wouldn't stand a chance.

"What choo want?" asked Scooter.

"What I want to know is why you're following me?" said Wil. "In this country ya gotta be real careful who's behind ya."

"I thought you was a friend of mine."

"Well, I'm not. You been messin' with my traps?" asked Wil.

"Naw. I don't mess wit nobody's stuff."

Wil saw that the man was slowly moving his rifle barrel toward him so he could get a quick shot. Wil pulled back his coat so that the man could see his Colt. Then he backed off some and started to grin. He had long black hair and reminded him of someone he had worked with at one time.

"I'm headed for da Injun camp a few miles from here." said

Scooter.

"What's yur name?"

"Pierre Matte'." said the man. "I from Canada."

With that Wil backed off some and dropped his guard. He had many friends among the Canadians.

"Well Pierre, I'm sorry I mistook you for trouble. You go your way and I'll go mine."

With that the two parted company, each going a different direction. Then Wil stopped and watched as the man walked away, not wanting to take his eyes off him. When he had gotten nearly 50 yards away, the man turned quickly and went to lift his rifle, but he saw that Wil was still watching him so he waved and kept on walking. When the man was out of sight, Wil continued along his trail, picking up his empty traps. Still he was thinking that he knew the man. His French Canadian accent too made him try hard to think who it could be. He was sure he knew this man, but the face wasn't familiar to him. A chill went up his back and a spark of recognition grew into a bright flame. It was Scooter, the man who burned out the Anderson's and tried to kill him in the woods right after the fire. Brad Sherman, B.S., Scooter, all the same, this was the man. Wil had his chance to get him and messed it up. Just the same, he got away without getting killed too.

The next day Wil sent a message to the Sheriff in International Falls and said that he would like to talk to him about Scooter. The Sheriff showed up not too many hours later in his shiny black Ford.

"What do you know Wil?" asked the Sheriff.

Wil told him the story about how they met and the rest of the circumstances. Then he told about how the man said he was heading for the Ojibwe camp past the big pines. Wil wasn't sure about that part, but it could have been where Scooter had been hiding, riding out the winter. There had been no murders for quite a while so he was getting food somehow.

# CHAPTER 11
## THE HUNT

Scooter made it back to the Indian camp and went inside his lodge. There was an older Indian woman breast feeding a baby. He gave a great yell that he wanted something to eat and when the woman didn't move fast enough, he grabbed her by the hair and yelled in her face to get him some food. The baby started to cry and the woman laid him down by the fire to stay warm.

She went and found a frying pan and started cooking some kind of meat. Then she warmed up some fry bread for him. Scooter had been providing food by robbing Wil's trapline. His food was whatever Wil had trapped. This was how he managed to survive. He had moved in on a small band of Ojibwe and killed their old chief and took his woman. Now he had the rest of them so scared that they did whatever he told them. They all feared for the lives of their families.

He was a bad man and they wanted to be rid of him. One of the young men planned to kill him and thought he could get him when he came outside in the morning to relieve himself, when he was still sleepy.

The next morning the man took his hunting bow and hid behind the shack that Scooter was in. The cold was deep and penetrating and it made him shiver. The sun was starting to rise, and he heard the sound of a door opening. He got ready and looked around the corner, shaking from fear or cold, uncertain from which it came. He saw Scooter and brought his bow to full draw. He loosed the arrow, right into Scooter. The man yelled and turned to see the face of his attacker, a young boy of only 15 summers. Scooter ran at him with his knife drawn. He grabbed the boys long hair, pulled back his head and cut the boy's throat, letting the life blood run out on the freshly fallen snow. Scooter stood watching as the boy flopped around in his final moments. He was thinking that it looked a lot like when he would kill a chicken.

The arrow had went into his shoulder and all the way through to the other side. He broke it off and pulled out the shaft that was left. He stumbled into the lodge yelling at the woman to get him some bandages. She did what she was told and wrapped him up, putting a large amount of skunk grease on the wound. She walked outside to see what had happened and found her own son lying dead in the snow. He had been trying to save his mother and lost his life in the process. Deep inside she wanted to mourn, to cry out loud, to let Gitche Manitou, the Great Spirit know how sad she was, but she made no sound for fear of her life and the life of the child. She walked back inside and lifted her baby to her breast and fed him.

The Sheriff stopped at the General Store and talked to Milo for a while. He wanted that man in custody before he could kill again. He had a good idea where Scooter was and thought that if he could gather enough men, they could catch him unaware. If they came at him in the middle of the night, he'd have nowhere to run. While they talked, Wil came in and joined the conversation. They made a plan to take a dozen men, including themselves, and to do it quickly before he could get away.

The plan was set. The Sheriff picked up the men he needed and deputized them all in Milo's store at midnight. Then by truck he took the whole group to a place not far from the Indian camp. They were as quiet as could be and when they entered the village everyone was still asleep. The Sheriff had no idea which lodge Scooter was in so he decided to enter the first one quietly and see who was inside.

He pushed open the door and shined his light into the faces of the awakening people. It wasn't the right place. Then he tried another and was greeted by a large dog barking loudly. The people scrambled to their feet and he could see that this wasn't the right one either, but he asked and was told which lodge to look in.

Scooter awakened to the sound of the barking dog and looked outside to see what was happening. He saw the men a short way off and in the moonlight saw their guns. He grabbed his coat and slipped on his moccasins. Then he took his rifle and went outside through the window. He took his snowshoes and disappeared into the night.

He had only been gone a couple minutes and the men were there with guns drawn. They heard the baby crying and came in like a flood. The old woman was holding the child and it was clear that nobody else was there. The window was open and Scooter had once again beaten the law. There was no way that they could catch him, especially at night on snowshoes. The Sheriff had to admit that he had been beaten again by Scooter.

The search for this murderer took on a whole new pace with the killing of the young Indian boy. He seemed capable of nearly anything. He called on the Bureau of Criminal Apprehension in Minneapolis to aid with Scooter's capture. After a few weeks of chasing him around the countryside, the attempts to capture him became fewer and far between. The Sheriff was sure he would show up again, but not sure where or when.

Scooter, in the dark of night, moved back across the river into Canada. He could breathe somewhat easier there but still had a hard time finding enough food to live on. Near the small town of Emo, he found a woman that was willing to take him in for the winter. They drank a lot and fought over nearly anything, but this woman was different, she refused to back down to his loud voice and violent nature.

The winter was passing slowly and Scooter was completely out of beer money. One evening late at night he was prowling the vacant streets of Emo looking for a drunk to roll or something to steal to keep him going. Somewhere around midnight, he found what he was looking for, a drunk walking in an alley. He came up behind him and hit him on the back of his head, knocking the victim to the ground. He went through the man's pockets and found a large amount of cash. There were several hundred dollars and he took it all. Then he disappeared into the night.

The next day, the Mounties were going from door to door asking if anyone had seen or heard anything around midnight last night. Scooter's woman answered the door as he hid in the bedroom.

"Did you see anything last night around midnight?" asked the Mountie.

"Nope. I was sleeping all night."

"Are you positive?"

"Yah. I went to bed around nine."

"Well, the president of the bank got killed somewhere around midnight and whoever it was took all his money," he said. "Well, if you hear anything, let us know. Eh?"

The Mountie went to get back in his car and saw the fresh tracks in the snow. It had snowed around midnight and then quit. There were tracks in the snow near her house going into the back door, tracks made after midnight. He thought to confront the woman again, but wanted to get some extra help with this one so he drove to the station.

Scooter came out and looked a bit worried. He had watched the Mountie examining the tracks and knew he would be back with reinforcements. He put on his clothes and checked his pockets for the money. He opened the door and walked outside, right toward the river. As he went over the hill, he turned to look back and the police cars were already heading toward the house. Scooter moved downhill and out onto the ice of the river. The United States was only a short distance away and the Mounties would never cross the border. He felt safe once again.

He caught a ride to International Falls and changed some of his money into U.S. funds. He had enough now to last him quite a while. He checked into a hotel and tried hard to change his appearance once again. He bathed and bought new clothes. Then he went to the barber shop for a short haircut and a neatly trimmed beard. So far everything was working out for him. He looked in the mirror and approved of the transformation.

It was still cold but spring weather was only a short way off. Then he would head south and find a good place to spend his money. His newfound wealth nearly made him giddy. Evenings he would head to the nearby saloon and drink until he could hardly stand. He was making an impression on some of the area toughs as being a free spender.

Then one evening, as he headed back to his hotel room, he ran into a couple of men in an alley and they beat him and took nearly all of his money. He lost several hundred dollars and all that remained of his ill gotten gain was $5.00 he had left in his other pants pocket. Broke once again, he checked out of his hotel room and left International Falls for the lumber camps. It was nearly spring, and they were letting men go. He would see if there was a card game or maybe somebody that he could rob. There was a lot of money in those pockets.

Life was slowing down some in the R and H camp. They had seen a good season and it looked like everyone was going to make some money this year. They had no serious accidents and the men's families would be glad to see them after so long. They had their landings full of big, red pine logs, waiting for the river to open. Then the river pigs would run them all to the big mills.

Sam and Missy invited Ma, Wil, Peter, and Mary Jane to a special dinner at the camp one evening at the end of the season. There were also a few of their closest lumberjack friends, and to top off the evening Mr. Withers would be there too. He seemed to be pretty happy with the first year's tally and wanted them all to know it.

Scooter had found another victim and killed him for his years wages near the R and H camp. The style of the crime once again brought in the Sheriff and some deputies. They had an area surrounded that they were sure contained the murderer. It was nearly 20 square miles, but they had tracked him into the spot and had asked for some bloodhounds from Minneapolis to come to help him.

The dogs arrived the next morning and the handlers on horseback did their best to keep up with them. In the course of the morning the dogs seemed to be getting more anxious about the trail. They bayed loudly sometimes when they would catch Scooter's scent.

They stopped for lunch around midday and ate a hurried sandwich. The whole crew was still pretty agitated and wanted to get right back on the trail. By three p.m. the dogs had outdistanced the men by quite a way. Bogs and marshes were hard to run a horse through. Then near dark, they came upon the body of one of the dogs. His skull was caved in and it looked like he had gotten a bit too close to Scooter. The other dogs were still in that same area, milling around, not quite knowing what to do. The handlers gathered them in and made camp for the night.

Next morning they picked up the trail again and the dogs howled with delight when they picked up his scent once again. Scooter was running hard, and they weren't exactly sure where he was headed, much less where they were. It seemed impossible that he could run this far without the dogs catching up to him, but he was a tough man and his freedom or maybe his life was at stake. They had been trailing him for several hours but now it seemed that they were on a hotter trail than they had been before. The dogs kept baying loudly and the men on horseback tried hard to keep up with them.

Last evening they had stopped for the night and that gave Scooter time to get way out ahead of them. Tonight they would continue the search, at least as long as the dogs would last. Milo from the General Store was one of the men in the posse and he thought that they were headed for the new R and H Lumber Camp on the river.

The whole group was sitting to dinner and enjoying the many stories and the good meal that Missy and Mary Jane had prepared for them. Mr. Withers had made a short speech and they all seemed to really like him. He was determined to make them all rich people and so far they were doing pretty well.

Outside in the dark, Scooter was a short distance in front of the bloodhounds and running hard in spite of near exhaustion. He ran up to the cook shack and found a window partially open and dove inside, trying hard to be quiet. It was Missy and Peter's room and right away he saw the small pistol that they had on the night stand.

Out in the dining room, they were all quietly eating their dessert when Missy heard something and excused herself to see what it was. She grabbed a lantern as she walked toward her room. When she opened the door, the light from the lantern shone brightly on the face of the man who had killed her family. It was the face in the window that had scared her so badly several years ago.

As soon as Scooter saw her, he grabbed for the pistol. Missy screamed loudly, yelling "It's him! It's him!" and dropped the lantern to the floor. It immediately broke open and spilled the coal oil all over the floor, catching the whole place on fire. Scooter tried hard to get to the window but his clothes were now on fire. Sam grabbed a bucket of water and threw it on him but there was little that could be done. He was writhing in flames, making no sounds as the flames consumed him. The whole place caught fire and was totally destroyed in a matter of fifteen minutes.

Sam, Missy, and the rest sat outside after the fire had nearly gone out. She was talking and Ma was crying. After being silent so long, Missy had a lot to say. Peter hugged her hard, glad that they were all still alive.

As they sat there, a dog came into the camp barking loudly, followed by another, and then a whole posse of men on horseback. The Sheriff walked up to the group and asked about the fire.

Several weeks had gone by and Missy was chattering a mile a minute and Peter was starting to wonder if she would ever take a deep breath. Everyone was getting settled into a more comfortable life on the river and there was no longer a reason to be fearful at night.

Wil never did get his old Colt back but the new one suited him fine. He carried it nearly all the time. This was a tough land and a man never knew when he might need a gun.

# Check out these other
# Great Books by Ron Shepherd

For More information on these books
and any upcoming books visit us at www.ronshepherd.com